RAGING BARONS MC

Book One – Truth and Lies
Prequel to Raging Barons MC

J.E. Daelman

COPYRIGHT © 2021 J.E. DAELMAN

All rights reserved

This book is a work of fiction. Names, characters, and events are the product of the author's imagination or have been used fictitiously. Do not construe them as real. Any resemblance to actual events or persons, living or dead, is purely coincidental.

This book or any portion thereof may not be reproduced or used in any manner whatsoever without the express written permission of the author. You cannot give for free on any kind of internet site.

This book is for readers over the age of 18 years. If bad language, violence, sexual encounters offend you, please do not read.

There may be mention of physical violence, torture, or abuse, but the series is a lighter version of MC. Hence, for example, rape *will never* be described in the series but may be mentioned.

Cover Designer: Oasis Book Covers

Editor: R. Tonge

Alpha Reader: M. D Vayer [USA]

Beta Readers: K. Perez [USA] S. Simanska [USA] V. Saunders [UK] E. Frost [UK]

Note

Please note, this author lives in the United Kingdom and has American Alpha and Beta readers who correct errors, but, as in other countries, it depends on which state you live as to how your slang or terms differ.

Therefore, although some words/terms you may think are incorrect are correct in one or more states.

REGISTERED

IF YOU HAVE NOT PURCHASED THIS COPY YOU NEED TO DELETE THE FILE AS IT IS STOLEN. PLEASE RESPECT THE AUTHORS RIGHT TO EARN AN HONEST LIVING.

You can read for free on Amazon with Kindle Unlimited

TABLE OF CONTENTS

COPYRIGHT © 2021 J.E. DAELMAN

NOTE

REGISTERED

TABLE OF CONTENTS

CHAPTER ONE

CHAPTER TWO

CHAPTER THREE

CHAPTER FOUR

CHAPTER FIVE

CHAPTER SIX

CHAPTER SEVEN

CHAPTER EIGHT

CHAPTER NINE

CHAPTER TEN

CHAPTER ELEVEN

CHAPTER TWELVE

CHAPTER THIRTEEN

CHAPTER FOURTEEN

CHAPTER FIFTEEN

CHAPTER SIXTEEN

CHAPTER SEVENTEEN

CHAPTER EIGHTEEN

CHAPTER NINETEEN

CHAPTER TWENTY

CHAPTER TWENTY-ONE

CHAPTER TWENTY-TWO

CHAPTER TWENTY-THREE

CHAPTER TWENTY-FOUR

BOOKS BY J.E. DAELMAN

ACKNOWLEDGEMENTS

YOU CAN FIND ME HERE:

CHAPTER ONE

-:- MIA -:-

Walking away from the prison where I've been for the last five years, serving a sentence for stabbing a woman who was hurting Zara, my man's daughter, who was only seven years of age at the time. I beat the hell out of Cara, and when she lifted the blade, I managed to get it off her, and yep, I stabbed the bitch, quite happily. Lucky for me, I suppose, I didn't kill her, but it got me the time.

The lies that bitch told were staggering, and the sad thing was she was believed. Brad 'Gunner' Michaelson was my man. He should have known me better.

He knew Cara was low life scum who got pregnant by poking holes in the condoms. Well, he can have her for eternity as I won't be going back.

Lifting my backpack onto my shoulder, I take the first steps of my freedom away from everything I ever knew and start walking away from this hell and toward my future.

Climbing onto the bus provided by the prison service to the halfway house, I sit near the window, looking out over the landscape. I press my forehead to the glass and close my eyes for a moment, thanking God I survived.

No one will know I was called 'Blade' inside because of what I'd done, and they don't know I had fashioned one as protection inside, but the ones that tried to do me over soon learned to stay away.

Checking how many dollars I have gives me a sense of safety as I earned quite a bit while incarcerated—working hard, keeping my head down, living one day at a time. That is what I'll continue to do, live one day at a time and move forward.

~~~~

Six Weeks Later

Serving at the local diner, I'm rushing back and forth to tables as we are in rush hour. Suzie is behind the counter today, and Graham is in the kitchen cooking up a storm.

These two have been married for seventeen years, and you can see they still love each other deeply. They started the diner as they didn't want to spend time apart, and this was an easy way for them to work together.

Suzie is around five-three, has dark collar-length hair, brown eyes, a real sweet personality. Graham is five-eleven, shaved head, has blue eyes, pretends to be a grump, but he's a kind man, but not a fool.

I've been lucky that Suzie and Graham took me on and have allowed me to rent the small apartment above the diner. It also helps them as they can call on me if they get unexpectedly busy. I'm always going to help them as they are helping me.

After settling into my job, I purchased new clothing and dyed my hair black but kept the waist-length in a braid. The property patch tattoo on my shoulder I had covered with a black rose with three red tears leaking from it. I keep it covered at all times. It's my reminder that you can trust no one as they will stab you in the heart the first chance they get.

"Mia, table six order ready," Suzie shouts.

Picking up the two plates, I hurry and carry them to the table where two men are sitting. I had not noticed them come in and order. I must have been on my ten-minute break

Placing the plates in front of these two, I keep my head down as they are wearing MC kuttes. I try and see the name of the MC, but without stopping, I can't read it.

"Thanks, doll." one of them murmurs, smiling at me. I return it and quickly walk away.

Keeping one eye on them, I make sure I stay busy and hope they don't hang around too long. I think I recognize one as Crack, the Enforcer of the club Gunner belonged to, but without looking right at him, I'm not sure.

As they stand to leave, I see the back of their kuttes, Rogue Legion MC. I walk through the kitchen, keeping my head down and side-eye Suzie, who sees me scurrying away.

"Have a nice day now," Suzie calls to them as they open the diner door and leave.

Leaning against the wall in the back hall, I struggle to get my breathing under control. Shit, that was close; the last thing I want is them finding me, now or ever.

Calming myself, I head back to the diner, clear tables, and serve the last lunchtime customers. As the afternoon rolls through, I find myself settling back down again.

The rest of the day flies past, and once Suzie has the main door to the diner locked, we all work together to clean the kitchen thoroughly. This is not part of my job, but I always help them. They are the only people to have shown me kindness in over five years.

Once done, Suzie takes out the three plates she always has for us, and we take our seats near the register wall. I know it's coming. I can feel it.

"Okay, Mia, I think it's time you told us what happened to you and why you nearly shit your panties when you saw those two bikers," Graham states gently.

Sitting back in my seat, I take a sip of my coffee and let my mind wander back nearly six years.

"I was in a relationship with a biker called Gunner. He was part of the Rogue Legion MC. I won't get into it all but know that he had a daughter with a club whore, and she walked out when Zara was born. When Zara was two, Gunner and I started seeing each other. I wasn't part of the club. I worked in the town bank at the time," I walk over to the counter and pick up the coffee pot and top us all off, "Long story short, Cara came back, attacked Zara, and I beat on her, she pulled out a knife, and I managed to get it off her and stabbed her. She told everyone that I was jealous of her and that I had been beating Zara, she tried to stop me, and I stabbed her. I wasn't believed, so I was arrested, found guilty, and imprisoned for five years. Now I don't want anything to do with any of them."

"Oh Mia, they don't deserve you anyway," Suzie murmurs. She wraps her arms around me and hugs me tightly.

"Fuckin' bitch. I hope the truth will come out one day, Mia. It has a way of doing that when you least expect it." Graham picks my hand up and squeezes it gently.

"I did time, Graham, not my time, but I did it. I learned a lot inside, and now I can look after myself. I will always love you both for helping me when no one else wanted to." I state, giving them both a warm smile. "I don't want them to find me; it's one of the reasons

I dye my hair, to make me less noticeable as Miriam, which is my real name. But I'm now Mia and Blade to those inside that kept away from me."

"Can you change your name legally?" Suzie asks.

"Yes, but if I do, the tech man at the MC will easily find out what I change it to and find me. So, I'm not going to do that. I'll just stay as Mia and work for cash in hand. I'll stay here with you as long as they don't find me." I state, then pick up the dishes and take them into the kitchen.

"You can stay here as long as you like, Mia. These people don't deserve you anyway. We want you to stay with us, and if they come in again, you can disappear up to your apartment if you need to." Graham says as he places his arm around my shoulders, pulling me into a hug.

The next few weeks pass with no sightings of the Rogue Legion MC. I know better than to relax, and although I'm five towns over from their clubhouse, it still means I need to be alert if I leave the safety of the diner.

Washing down all the tables, I'm tired and ready to be closing the door anytime. Suzie is cashing out the register, and Graham is starting to switch off stoves and close out the kitchen for cleaning.

As I finish the last table, the door opens, and four men walk in, talking loudly, and they throw themselves onto a back table.

I give Suzie a look as we notice they are wearing the MC kutte. Fuck I need to keep my head, stay calm, and ride this out. I'm pleased I had re-colored my hair two days back, and the natural auburn color no longer showed through at the roots. The green contacts Graham suggested I wear also help as my warm chocolate brown could have caused some recognition.

Picking up my waitress pad and pencil, I walk over with the coffee pot and cups on a tray.

"Coffee?" I state in a bored tone.

"Thanks, doll." one of them responds, but I don't look up, preferring to keep my eyes down. I place cups out and fill them, then take the pot and tray before walking back again, "What can I get you all?"

"What you got left, babe?" one of them asks, looking at his kutte. He's VP and called Trip. I never knew this man, thankfully.

"We can make y'all a fry up, bacon, eggs, sausage, hash browns, mushrooms, and toast," I state, keeping my voice as bored sounding as possible.

"Yeah, that will do doll, four of those." the one at the back of the table states, looking up, he is staring at me intently, flicking my eyes down, he's the Enforcer, Crack it says on his kutte, he was part of the MC when I was with Gunner and I don't want him to recognize me. I didn't have anything to do with many at the club, and I hope that works for me.

Crack is six-two, well built, short brown hair, and a beard. If I remember rightly, he was a reasonably okay guy.

"Okay, it'll be about twenty minutes." and I walk back to the kitchen, giving Graham the order.

Graham leans over and whispers to me, "Go to your apartment. If they ask, I'll say it was your knock-off time. They won't know you're in the apartment above."

I nod and quickly but quietly climb the back stairs to my apartment and close the door, leaning against it taking in deep breaths, trying to calm my racing heart. Shit is getting too close, and maybe I need to leave soon.

I walk into the bedroom and open the top drawer in the dresser and count the dollars I've managed to save so far. Seven hundred, not going to get me far. I need to keep saving.

Looking around, the bedroom is not large, but it's clean, tidy and it's got a bed, dresser, bedside table, and a small chair.

The kitchen is small and has a sink, small fridge, stove, microwave and lastly a utility with a washer and dryer. The lounge is larger, has a couch, TV, and coffee table. The bathroom has a sink with a cabinet under it, toilet, and shower unit, nothing flashy but fair condition.

I can cope with living here nicely, after being in prison for five years., this is pure luxury. The MC gutted out the apartment I had before prison, I presume. No one ever came to see me or tell me where my things were. At first, it hurt me that I had lost all that I had worked for, and then to lose what I thought was my family has left me bitter, and I won't ever trust again.

I quickly shower and change, placing my work clothes in the washer, sitting down to dry my hair which takes forever with it being so long and thick. This relaxes me, and I start to feel the tension in my shoulder leave.

With a soft tapping on the apartment door, I walk over and open it to see Suzie. She smiles and steps inside. Taking the brush from my hand, I walk into the lounge and sit again. Suzie picks up the dryer and starts to dry and brush my hair.

"They've gone obviously, and they didn't ask where you had gone or even look for you that I could see. I kept one eye on them Mia, but they showed no sign of interest," after another few minutes, Suzie takes a deep breath, "Do you think they are actively looking for you? Do you think they know you're out of prison now?"

"I don't know, Suzie. No one was at the gate when I was released. I took the bus to the halfway house, and I never saw any of them." I respond, running my hands up and down my thighs with nerves. "If they look like they're getting aware, I'll move on. I won't put you in any danger."

"You will not. We don't want you moving on anywhere, and if they start trouble, we'll go to the cops. You served your time, and as you said, Mia, not even your time. I won't have you run off." Suzie is pissed, something I've never seen or heard from her before. She is such a calm, caring person, and her anger has taken me by surprise.

"Let's just keep calm about it, Suzie. If they keep coming in and show any interest, then we can revise what to do. So far, it seems they are calling in on their way back from somewhere, rather than looking for anything." I tell her, braiding my hair and then taking Suzie's hand and giving it a light squeeze.

Once Suzie has left, I make a hot chocolate and pick up my kindle, which I take to my bedroom and sit on the bed leaning on the headboard. As the room darkens, I don't put the lamp on as I feel nervous and don't want anyone to know the apartment is in use. I get ready for bed in the dark after double-checking the apartment door lock and settling down for the night.

CHAPTER TWO

-:- MIA -:-

One of the jobs at the diner that I most detest is cleaning the toilets. People are so disgusting it makes you want to vomit. Toilet paper all over the floor, water splashed everywhere, the soap dispenser hanging off again. The things to sort are never-ending in here.

Grabbing a pair of gloves, I set about cleaning all the toilets. The industrial cleaners always make my eyes water, so I don't usually wear my contacts, but for some reason, I decided to keep them in today.

I have my earbuds in and listening to some rock music, I'm not up to date with the newer groups, but I'll enjoy listening to them and working out which ones I like the best.

Once I have the toilets cleaned, I start mopping out the stalls, and then I'll move on to clean the urinals. Men stink. Can they never piss straight?

Finishing the urinals, I set about cleaning the sinks and mirrors. My mind is miles away, trying to work out how much I can save from my next paycheck.

Someone taps me on the shoulder, and I spin around and smash out with the heel of my hand and hit someone in the nose. A loud "What the fuck!" is snarled, and I step back when I see it is a man with a kutte. This man is around six-two, dark hair in a man bun, close shaved beard, very handsome, kill me now is my thought.

"Oh, I'm so sorry, you scared me," I say, trying to sound like a weak little lady.

"I'm sorry too, I didn't mean to frighten you, I just wanted to take a piss and was letting you know I was here," he states, and that's when I notice his kutte says President - Axel.

"It's okay, I'll go stand outside until you're finished." and I try to get out of the bathroom fast, but he reaches out and takes hold of my arm.

"Do I know you?" he asks, frowning at me.

"No, I don't think so." I pull my arm away and quickly go out and to the kitchen, holding a hand on my chest, deep breathing to try and get myself under control.

Graham looks up and frowns, but I shake my head and nod to the bathroom down the corridor.

I stand and wait, leaning on the wall, doing my best to look like I'm bored waiting to get back to work.

The man named Axel comes out of the bathroom, nods, and walks past me back into the dining area. As I watch him pass, I turn and see the back of his kutte, which has the logo Raging Barons MC.

My heart settles down now I know they're not the MC I have to stay hidden from. But one thing is for sure I don't want to get mixed up with another MC ever.

I return to the bathroom and finish up as fast as I can. The urgency to get back to the apartment is snapping at me. I need to get behind a closed door and feel safe for a while.

As I pass the kitchen, Suzie shouts to me, so I turn and pop my head in, asking, "You okay, Suzie? Do you need something?"

"We have a full house Mia, could you help out? I don't want you to be put in a position, but I'm falling behind. It's not the ones who you're worried about." Suzie states giving me a hopeful look.

"Shit Suzie," I say. "Okay, but if it looks like trouble, I'm outta here."

"Thanks, Mia."

I owe these two people such a lot I don't have a problem helping them. It's the current customers that are the problem. Sucking it up, I grab my apron and head into the diner, Graham giving me a thank you look on the way past.

Shit, the place is packed with MC men. I take a breath and head to the first table, "What can I get y'all?"

Taking the order, I hand it to Suzie, who pins it up for Graham, then I take the following table, and that is all I do, keep my head down, take orders, give out meals, top-up drinks, I say as little as possible.

I don't recognize any of these men, so they shouldn't recognize me, especially with my different hair color and contacts. I don't remember mixing with this club when I used to go to the clubhouse with Gunner.

Thankfully, no problems arise, but I note that the President Axel has been watching me work. I'm sure I don't know him, and I think with his six-foot four-inch height, I would remember.

They all seem to have eaten, so I start clearing tables and topping up any cups. I hand out their checks as I go along. One of them grabs hold of my wrist as I reach to pick up dirty plates, and I rotate my hand from left to right, which makes him lose his grip.

I jump back from the table, and I have my blade strapped to my calf if I need it. Thankfully my loose pants keep it from being obvious.

"Keep your hands off, Knuckle, or you'll answer to me." the President has stood and is walking over towards us. I back off, not wanting to get close to anyone. "Sorry, he'll be spoken to once we get him back to the clubhouse. Are you okay?"

"I'm fine, thank you." I step back even further, then I feel someone at my back, but before I react, Graham steps in front of me.

"Time to leave, boys. Come back anytime when your boy here has learned his manners." Graham keeps his calm and speaks only to the President.

"No trouble here, we'll be back when passing, and he'll have manners," Axel responds, nodding to them all to head out the door.

They all leave the diner, and Axel throws down a couple of hundred dollars, nodding at Graham, and closes the door as he leaves.

I stand until they have all left the parking lot in front and then sit heavily at one of the tables. Suzie rubs her hand over my shoulder and squeezes it.

"Did you know any of them, Mia?" Graham asks, sitting opposite me.

"No, I didn't recognize any. I don't think I've seen that MC before." I pinch the top of my nose with my thumb and forefinger, trying to relieve some of the stress.

"The one who paid, with President on his jacket, kept looking at you." Suzie murmurs, frowning with some worry, "He either thought he knew you, or he liked the look of you."

"Christ, I hope not. I don't want anything to do with any MC. I know Nevada has a few MCs around and Montana. Those are the states these two clubs come from, so unless I move totally out of the way, I think there'll always be one." I state.

"Do you ever think of clearing your name Mia?" Graham asks, placing an iced tea in front of us all.

"Not really, Graham. I don't think there's any way I can do that. Cara would never admit to lying, and no one ever asked me what happened. They all just believed her. Even Zara didn't say anything, and she was seven, as I told you. She could have told them I didn't hurt her." That's what hurts me more than even Gunner never asking me what happened.

I'd helped everyone in that club one way or another, from babysitting to shopping when they were ill, driving them if they didn't have a vehicle, cleaning the bar, and even cooking up meals now and again.

Five years inside, I still don't understand how any of them could believe I would hurt Zara when she was like a daughter to me. I'll never forgive them, and one day I hope Cara and Gunner will both get what karma throws at them.

-:- CRACK -:-

Sitting in Church, I look around at my brothers, and I'm not sure I should bring up the subject I'm about to as it has been a topic no one wanted to talk about for the last five years.

We discuss the run we just finished and the upcoming business. The coffers are in good shape for this time of the year. Two new prospects were voted to try out, both being relatives of brothers of the club.

Sharp, our President for the last eight years, is trying to get the club clean, and we are getting to that point. We just have to sidestep gently from some of our oldest customers.

"Any other business?" Sharp asks as he lifts his gavel.

"Yeah, I have something I want to discuss," I add before I change my mind.

"Okay, Crack, what do you want to discuss?" Sharp says, leaning back in his seat.

"Everyone here remembers Miriam," this has the room bursting into grumbles, snarls, and deadly remarks, "Hang on, let me speak." I snarl, "Does anyone know when her time was gonna be up?"

"Anytime this year." Gunner snarls, "When she gets out, I'm gonna kill her if I find her."

"You know what, Gunner? I never believed what was said. Miriam loved you and Zara. We all could see that. I don't think for a minute she would hurt anyone, let alone that little girl. Now Cara, yeah, that bitch would, and you never even spoke to Miriam to find out the truth. You also made sure none of us got to speak to her either. If she didn't do this, she's served five years for something she didn't do." I state, giving him it straight. He should have had her back, found out at least what she had to say.

"What? Did you want to fuck her Crack? Did you want in her panties?" Gunner snarls.

"You are disgusting, Gunner. She's better off without you. If I ever find her, I'm gonna ask her what happened. I'm gonna find out if Cara lied, and if she did, you can believe she'll be in the fuckin' shed." after slamming my hands on the table, I walk out, pissed off, and make sure I shoulder slam Gunner as I walk past him.

-:- ZARA -:-

Knowing I shouldn't, I listen in on what is being said in Church. I've gotten into the habit of listening since I was attacked when I was seven. I know where the air vent is, and you can hear everything clearly.

I don't want to talk to anyone here. They never spoke to me about what happened, and they just listened to that bitch of a mother of mine. I hate her; she is a horrible person.

I'm scared of her, and she hits me when my dad isn't around, but never anywhere that will show bruises only on my body. I don't bother with my dad much anymore either. He's always so busy or trying to stay away from my mother that he ignores me most of the time too.

If Miriam is going to be around, I want to find her. She loved me. She used to sing to me, hug me and kiss me on the nose. They should all know, she wouldn't hurt me, I don't care what they all think anymore, I'm going to find her.

I've got savings now, and I'm not a baby anymore. I'm twelve, nearly thirteen. I'm going to find Miriam if I can. If I watch Crack and keep my ears open, I may know where to look. He didn't say everything he knew, I'm sure of it.

"Zara, where are you?" Cara is shouting. I refuse to call her mother even in my head: she doesn't deserve it. I'm gonna hide in my place until she's gone.

I look like Cara. I'm just over five foot at the moment, still may grow a little more, but she's five-three, so I think I'm going to be short like her. We have dark blonde hair, blue eyes, and freckles over our noses. My dad is six-foot-two, with short brown hair and brown eyes. I don't think I have any of his looks or traits as he is a hothead and stubborn.

"Zara, where are you?" I hear Cara shout again, but I slink away to my hiding place, no way am I going to her, she's a horrid mother and person.

CHAPTER THREE

-:- MIA -:-

Two days since the MC had been in, and I'm starting to relax again. I don't need the stress. I'll have to move again when I've saved up enough. I don't want to spend my life always looking over my shoulder, but what choice do I have.

Today is my day off, and I hope Suzie doesn't call me in to help out. I want to clean the apartment and do my laundry, I don't have much as I still only have three changes of clothes, but it's enough for now.

Mid-afternoon, I have everything cleaned, and laundry finished. Looking in my small fridge and cupboards, I think I better run over to the store and do a little shopping. I need to replace the few things that are low and maybe treat myself to something for breakfast for a change.

Eating the last meal with Graham and Suzie is good and saves me money, but I don't always want to eat with them. I can't afford to be too reliant on them or let them into my heart too far because when things go to shit, it will hurt, and it will go to shit. It always does.

Picking up my purse, I head downstairs, and as I pass the kitchen, Graham calls to me.

"Yeah, what's up, Graham?" I ask as I pop my head through the kitchen door.

"Are you goin' out, Mia?" Graham asks and steps towards me while holding a greasy-looking pan he's washing.

"Just over to the store. I won't be very long. Do you need anything while I'm out?" I ask him, making sure he can't get near enough to drop grease on my clothes.

"No, I don't think so. But you be careful. Keep your eyes peeled. I have a feelin', and I don't ignore it when I get twitchy." he says, which has me studying his face, and he looks a bit strained.

"Are you okay?" and as I ask, Suzie walks into the kitchen.

"Yes, I'm fine, we're fine, it's you I'm worried about." Graham states, looking over his shoulder at Suzie, "We care deeply about you Mia, we don't want anything to happen to you."

"If any trouble comes here, I'll leave. I won't bring it onto your heads. I care about you too, and I don't want anything to happen to you either."

"Just keep your eyes open; stay alert," Suzie says, taking my hand and squeezing it.

"I will." Leaving the diner to do my shopping, I keep my eyes open as I walk the short way down the street and then cross the road, seeing nothing and no one out of place.

Walking around the store, I pick up the items I need placing them in my cart, but I enjoy the time away from the diner, so I have slipped into a daydream.

Reaching the register, I place my items for the young woman to ring through. While I'm paying, I hear a familiar voice, and looking up, I see a reflection in the window of two bikers. Paying, I quickly walk out, keeping my eye on the window, and my heart is jumping nearly out of my chest

That was Gunner and Crack, the one that first came into the diner. I want to stay well away from all of them.

Keeping my head down, I quickly head back to the diner and around the back, entering through the back door of the kitchen.

Graham looks up and knows something is wrong and rushes over to me, "What? What is it, Mia?"

"Bikers in the store. One was Gunner, the one I was with, whose daughter I was accused of hurting. He was with one that was here the first time those bikers came in. I recognize him now, too; he's Crack the Enforcer of the club." I rush to say, keeping my voice down in case anyone hears in the diner.

"Go up to your apartment and stay there. If anyone asks, you're not around today." Graham pushes me towards the stairs, and I jog up them and lock myself in my apartment, taking a deep breath and praying I'm not found.

-:- CRACK -:-

Coming out of the store, I look across the road and remember the diner and the meal I had. "Great diner over the road, do you wanna go?" I ask Gunner, I'm still not back to normal with him, "They do some great food, and I'm fuckin' hungry."

"Yeah, why not, could eat something, sick of the swill Cara throws at me." Gunner moans, "I've been eating at the clubhouse when I can."

As we walk over to the diner, I think about Zara and have not seen her around for quite a while. "How's Zara? I haven't seen her around for ages."

"Fine as far as I know." Gunner replies, but he doesn't seem sure.

"What do you mean as far as you know?" I ask, not liking this at all.

"I've not been to the house in two weeks. I don't want to be around Cara. She's driving me crazy with her whining and moaning. She always wants more money or something. I'm keeping away from her." Gunner tells me looking pretty damn miserable, if I'm honest.

"So, you've not seen Zara? Her birthday's soon, isn't she gonna be thirteen? A damn teenager, she'll be a young lady before you know it." I say, trying to keep my voice even as I feel like swinging for him and his lack of concern.

"Yeah. She'll fly the nest before we know it," he replies just as we reach the diner.

Opening the door, we pick a table to keep our backs to the wall and look over the menu. As I look up, I notice the young woman is not around by the looks of it. She was a pretty thing. I wouldn't mind spending some time with her.

An older lady walks over with cups and coffee pot, filling them once she's placed them in front of us.

"What can I get you today?" she asks and sounds a bit nervous. Mind you, plenty of people are with us wearing our kuttes.

"I had chicken pot pie last time I came in. It was the shit. Do you have any today?" I ask her, and she gives me a slight smile.

"Yes, we have them today. What would you like with that?"

"Large portion of fries will do with that," I tell her and place my menu down.

"What about you?" She asks Gunner, giving him what looks like a wary look.

"I'll have the same," he tells her, without looking up. Then he throws his menu down, which has her jumping.

"No young lady today?" I ask her, giving her one of my winning smiles.

"Oh, no, not today." and before I can say anything else, she scuttles away and into the kitchen.

"Who you talkin' about?" Gunner asks.

"When I was in last time, there was a real pretty young woman serving. She took my eye." I tell him.

"You wanted in there?" he smirks at me, "Not seen you with the club whores of late."

"No, I'm lookin' for something special. Sick of the skanks, you can have them. I want someone worth having, someone who's not just a hole to stick it in." I state with an attitude.

"No such thing, Crack. It's just an illusion," he says, sounding jaded.

Oh, yes, there is. I know as I saw it in Miriam, she loved him and his girl. He was just too stupid to trust it and her. I'll kill Cara if I find out she lied, and I'm sure she did. My worry at the moment is where Zara is as she is usually around, and I've not seen her for days.

The rest of the meal passed quietly, the food is just as good as it was last time, and I'm sure I'll be calling in here often.

Once we've eaten, we head back to the clubhouse, and I hope an early night for me. I'm sick of all the shit and drama that kicks off lately.

-:- ZARA -:-

After sitting in the room watching Zip work his computers, I point at a laptop, and he nods yes, I can take it. I snatch it up and carry it to my secret room, which is in the loft area of the clubhouse. I can get to it through the storeroom upstairs, and if I put the hatch back into place, no one knows I'm up there.

Scrambling up, I make sure I close myself in, then go into the middle of the loft and sit, open the laptop and switch it on. I don't know much about computers, but I'm going to learn, and maybe I'm young, but I'm not stupid.

I've learned a lot watching Zip over the last few months. I write notes, so I don't forget things essential to finding when Miriam will leave prison.

I start to search newspapers from the time it all happened. Maybe I'll learn things that everyone was hiding from me at the time.

A couple of hours later, I'm tired. I crawl over to the pile of bedding I took from other people's beds at the clubhouse to make a type of bed for me to sleep on up here. I sit on the bedding and grab a protein bar from the box. I've been storing things to snack on and bottles of water, a couple of cans of soda too.

While eating my bar, I think about why dad isn't coming home anymore and why he doesn't want to see me or spend time with me. I didn't do anything wrong, but I feel like I'm being punished for something.

After the bar and a bottle of water, I curl up on the bedding and fall asleep.

CHAPTER FOUR

-:- MIA -:-

Three weeks since I'd seen Gunner and Crack in the store, and since then, I've kept inside the diner and on alert. I'm tired and stressed. All this is nearly worse than being in prison. That was bad enough watching my back all the time, keeping my nose clean as I didn't want to have my time extended.

I think Graham and Suzie are feeling it too, and I'm going to be ready to move on soon. I calculate another four weeks, and I'll have enough to travel to another state and rent somewhere small.

Heading downstairs to the diner to start my shift, I notice a few people eating, but not a crowd yet. I walk into the kitchen and clean up the sink area, place everything into the dishwasher and then grab the garbage bag that is nearly overflowing.

The breakfast crowd must have been good with the clearing up I've just done, and I know it will be hard on them both when I leave as they are relying on me more and more.

Opening the back door, I drag out the garbage bag and head for the dumpster. Struggling to lift it, I didn't hear anyone come up behind me and jump badly when someone takes the bag and throws it in.

Turning, I see Axel, the President that was in a few weeks ago. I swallow and stutter but manage to say thanks.

"You got anythin' else to go in?" Axel asks me.

"No, that's it, thank you again," I murmur, then turn to go back inside.

Axel takes hold of my bicep and turns me, "Are you sure I don't know you? I have a feeling I should."

"No, I don't know you. Maybe I remind you of someone?" I say, doing my best to keep my cool as I can't afford to drop myself in the shit.

Nodding, Axel gives me a slight smile then turns toward the other bikers waiting for him. I nod to them and then quickly enter the kitchen and lean my back against the door.

Graham lifts an eyebrow in question. I walk over to him and quietly tell him what happened outside. "Stay calm, and Mia, just act as though nothing about that bothered you."

I nod, then wash my hands and place my apron on, ready to start my shift in the dining area.

Suzie is working behind the counter, making fresh pots of coffee and placing dishes through the hatch for washing. I pat her shoulder to let her know I'm here, and I take over clearing dishes.

As I'm done, I take my pad and walk over to the MC guys and ask if they're ready to order and if they need a coffee top-up.

Axel points at his empty, so I top his up and then turn to check out all the others before taking out my order pad again.

Once I have everyone's orders, I quickly take them and hang them up for Graham. I take the couple of orders that are ready and walk over to the table with a family of four—smiling at the two kids and checking if they need anything else before heading back to the kitchen.

I keep myself busy and hope the MC guys don't stay all afternoon. There are eight of them in total, but none should know me as it's not an MC I have ever had any contact with.

By the end of the day, I'm tired and need to have a hot bath and a glass of wine, something I don't usually do, but after today I need something to relax with.

-:- AXEL -:-

There is something about this woman. I can't put my finger on it, but something pulls at me. I'm sure her hair is dyed, but the length of it looks natural. I don't know her, I don't think, but something tells me I know of her. My gut instincts are never wrong, and although I'm not feeling alarmed, I want to know why I feel like I need to unravel this puzzle.

Tapping my VPs boot with the toe of mine, he looks over, and I nod slightly towards the woman called Mia and murmur for him to take a snap on his cell.

When we're ready to leave, the woman called Mia is in the kitchen, and I can see her working at the sink through the hatch. I stand at the register and pay for our meals, thanking the woman.

Once we get to the parking lot, I take my helmet and turn to my VP, Drag and tell him to find out who she is and anything he can find on her.

Drag is a man that is always alert. He takes his VP responsibilities more than seriously. He's six-feet-four, has brown hair, beard which he shaves regularly, gets lazy, and grows back again.

"You know her Pres?" Drag asks, sending the image to our tech man Specs.

"No, but something about her tells me I need to know," I comment; throwing my leg over my bike, I sit but don't start the engine for a minute. "Remind me later what you know of that case where the Rogue Legion MC had one of their own sent down."

"Oh, I remember that. A lot was goin' around sayin' that she was set up, and her man didn't even ask her side of what happened. Basically, she was railroaded." Drag responds, shaking his head and frowning, "I'll speak to Specs about that too as I'm sure he can find something on it."

"We didn't have much to do with them at that time. Five years ago, I think it was, but we've touched with them more since. Sharp was President then, and I always thought he should have dug into it himself, but he was that busy gettin' them clean I think he missed stuff." I tell Drag, and I note the interest from the rest has peaked. "Come on, let's get back to the clubhouse."

-:- ZARA -:-

Sitting in the loft, I'm writing down what I'm finding on the internet from the newspaper reports about Miriam. The photographs of her in court have me crying. She looks so lost and sad. She'd lost a lot of weight too.

The other photographs show Cara dressed up like she's going out for the night, spotless and perfect. She doesn't look like someone stabbed her.

My father is giving evil looks at Miriam in the courtroom. I didn't think they could take photographs in court, but they did. They didn't allow Miriam to speak either, and her lawyer just said that she was not guilty but had nothing else to say; that couldn't be right.

I write down the lawyer's name and where he worked, and the prison name it says Miriam was going to be taken.

Closing out the laptop, I check how many snacks I have left and then open the hatch a little bit to listen if the coast is clear. I need to find some more drinks and what I can take from the kitchen as snacks. I also want to grab someone's cell, so I have to be extra sneaky this time.

Once clear of the loft, I sneak around to the back door of the clubhouse. No one is about now, so I quietly go to the kitchen door and listen as I don't want to meet anyone.

Turning the door handle, I squeal when a large hand lands on mine, and I spin around to see who it is.

"What you doing little girl?" Crack asks me, grinning at the fact he made me jump.

I shrug my shoulder to say nothing.

"Come on, in you go." Crack opens the door and pushes me inside, and I stop dead in my tracks when I see Cara sitting at the table with a bottle of vodka.

"Where the fuck have you been?" Cara snarls at me, staggering to stand, "Come here, we're goin' home."

I shoot behind Crack; I'm not going with her. No way, she'll punch me some more because I've been hiding for four days.

As she comes towards me, I rush for the back door, and as I get it open, she catches my shirt, dragging me back and knocking me to the floor.

"Hey, don't do that to her." Crack snarls, grabbing Cara, and as he does that, I bolt out the door and run as fast as I can back to my hiding place.

Once safely back with the hatch down, I lay on the bedding and close my eyes. My heart is beating fast, making me feel a bit sick. I need to find out where Miriam is. She'll keep me safe.

CHAPTER FIVE

-:- AXEL -:-

Walking into the clubhouse, I look around and see Buzz, my Enforcer, sitting at the bar talking to the prospect who's on duty behind the bar until whatever time he's told to finish.

Buzz is six-feet-five, built like a brick shithouse. He shaves his hair at the sides and longer on the top, sandy brown color, brown eyes, beard when he feels like one. He is easygoing, but as an Enforcer, he can knock a man out with one punch, broken a jaw or two in the past.

The clubhouse is an old superstore, two stories. We built rooms into the place to have a kitchen with a dining area, utility, Church, three offices, storage, bedrooms, bathrooms, and security room that oversees the property and businesses.

We own a garage, and a night club, all run by brothers and legitimate. Getting out of gun-running and drugs was the best thing this club ever did. We lost brothers through that shit, and in my mind, it was never worth it.

Sitting next to Buzz, I tap on the bar for Jig, the prospect, to give me a beer, then turn to look at the room. Jig is five-feet-eleven, dirty blond, blue eyes, and clean-shaven. He is keen to earn his patch and has done more than many prospects are expected to, and he'll easily win his full patch.

The place needs a woman's touch, I think to myself, the club pussy is not cutting it for me. They hardly do fuck all, just enough to keep them safe. It's maybe time I bring it to the table. They either pull their weight or walk. I don't care; I've not tapped any of them in a fuck of a long time.

"You okay, Pres?" Buzz looks over at me, brows furrowed.

"Sick of this shit, look at the place." I snarl, "I'm not happy at what I'm seeing. We worked hard to get this clubhouse, most of us worked two jobs, put up our life savings, and it looks like a shithole."

Buzz looks around, and I see the moment he sees what I'm seeing. Club pussy, laying around on the sofa naked, brothers lounging about looking bored. Dirty floor, garbage is thrown around, overflowing waste bins, it's all gone to shit, the place stinks.

I look at Buzz, and he nods at me, "Yeah, I see it. What we gonna do about it?"

"You're gonna call Church, first thing in the morning, make it nine, let's make the fuckers' sweat. We're pulling this shit together." Scanning the room once more, I know what I'm about to do will be worth it. "While we're in Church, get one of the prospects to collect all the whores up and put them in the first office. Prospects stay with them; whores don't touch fuckin' nothing."

Buzz nods finishes his drink, and walks away. I know he'll get everything sorted. He and I think alike. We've been best friends since we were kids. He'll back whatever I decide to do next.

Throwing the rest of my beer back, I nod at Jig and walk over to security. I want to know if Specs, our tech man, found anything yet on the Rogue Legion MC incident. For some reason, it's grating on my last nerve. I just can't remember all that happened, but I was shocked at the time that they never allowed the woman to speak, not even in court. It looked like she'd been railroaded, and it never sits pretty when that happens, especially to a woman that more than likely was innocent.

Walking in, Specs looks up and nods, "Hi, Pres, what can I do for you?"

"Did you find anything from the photo?" I sit on the only lounge chair in the room and look at the rows of monitors surveying the club, garage, and ink shop. Nothing seems out of place, so I lose interest fast.

"It's interesting. The image I got highly resembles the woman, but it's five years since that conviction, and people change a lot, especially in prison." Leaning over, Specs picks up a printout of the woman when she was sent down and hands it to me. "As you can see looking at the side by side, we have similarities, hair longer, different color, but the eyes are different, here they are brown and here they are green."

I study the two images and see what he means, but the mouth looks the same and the eyebrows, cheeks even. Yes, she is a bit older, but bodily they look similar, although she is much slimmer now. In fact, she looks like she needs a few good meals.

Turning to Specs, I hand him the images back, "What do you think?" I ask as I'm nearly sure it's the same woman.

"I think it's highly likely it's her." Specs nods at me, "She won't want her cover being blown, Pres. She'll be trying to build a new life for herself, and that's not gonna be easy. If you blow her cover, if it is her, she'll run. We don't know what Rogue Legion MC will do if they find her. The last thing we want is her death on our hands."

Nodding, I agree with him, but I want to know what the fuck happened. I don't know why; it's just eating at me.

"Any chance you can get the prison records? Find out what happened while she was inside?" turning towards the door as I start to leave.

"You know my name, right Pres?" Specs smirks, he loves a challenge, and I would put a bet on having the information by bedtime. "Of course, I can get the records."

Slapping him on the back, I walk out of security and tap and open PT's door, he's our secretary, and we call him PT which is short for 'paper trail' as he can find anything we need regarding the club.

"PT, Buzz is callin' Church first thing in the morning. I want you to have details on hand of when we went legit and how much we all forked out to get this clubhouse and the businesses." leaning on the door frame because I'm not going in and having Sunday brunch, "I want all the info on what rooms are used, by who, how many are empty, and every bit of info you have on the whores."

"Okay, Pres, I'll have that for the morning, anything else?" PT asks, and I smirk as he has his notebook out, jotting down what he needs to have at the ready.

"You remember when that other club had a woman sent down, and they didn't allow her to even speak to anyone?" I ask as I know PT was around at the time.

"Yeah, I do. My sister Glory worked with her at the bank. She was called Miriam something, I don't remember, but Glory said she would never have done it because she loved that man and kid." PT sits back in his chair, rubbing his hand on the back of his neck, "Glory was pissed as she tried to visit Miriam in prison, and it was blocked. She was told the woman wasn't allowed visitors, ever, so not to go back."

"Well, that's a fuck load of bullshit," I snarl, "So the MC put a block on her ever having her say. Her man needs puttin' down." I shake my head in disgust, "Ask your sister if she remembers anything else, anything at all?"

"Will do. What's got your interest in this Pres?" he asks me, half turning back to his desk and paperwork.

"It just feels wrong. I thought so at the time, but I'm not sure if I ever saw the woman apart from the newspaper reports. She is out, if it is her, and could be in danger." I state, then head out to the main room and get a shot of something strong.

-:- ZARA -:-

Two days in the loft, and I have eaten up all that was in the box. I know I'm going to have to get out and grab more food and water. I still need to get a cell from somewhere if I'm going to make a run for it and find Miriam.

Opening the hatch slightly, I listen for any talking or noise of someone walking around, anything, I don't want to be caught, if I have to go back home Cara will hit me again. I don't know what my tutor is doing because she can't have reported me missing and I've not done any lessons in three weeks.

Not hearing anything, I climb out, making sure the loft hatch closes, and I sneak down the corridor. One of the bedroom doors is open, and as I pass, I see nobody is inside, yet a cellphone is sitting on the bed. I rush in, grab the cellphone and dash down the corridor, shoving it into the back pocket of my jeans.

Peeking into the kitchen, I wait a minute to make sure no one is around, then I bolt for the pantry door and get in, closing the door behind me.

I know where the chocolate bars are, so I grab a few and push them into my shirt, which I tucked into my jeans and buttoned so nothing will fall out.

Picking up some crackers, chips, and a couple of bottles of water, I know I can't carry anymore, so I open the door slightly and listen once again.

Hearing someone talking, I wait, leaning up against the wall just inside the pantry. I can hear they're talking about one of the women and something about her having a good mouth! That's a bit odd, but I've seen some things I shouldn't, so maybe it's a thing about sex!

As soon as they leave the kitchen, I bolt for the corridor and my safe place. I want to make sure that I get safely locked up as it's dark outside, and I need to check the time. Most men will hang around with the women once it's dark, and I don't want to be caught.

Safely back in the loft, I refill my box and open a bottle of water, sipping it to help it last longer. I look at the cell and see it has everyone's number in it, so it's got to be one of the men's cells.

Checking my notes, I ring the prison as I want to know if Miriam is still locked in that place. Thinking about it has my eyes watering. I wish someone would have listened to me.

"Baywater Elite Correctional Center, how can I help you?" a man's voice asks.

As I open my mouth to speak, all that comes out is a squeak. I cough to let him know I'm here and try again, "Can you tell me if Miriam is still there, please?" which comes out a bit ragged, but at least I said it.

"I'm sorry, Miriam, who?" he asks.

I check what my notes say, "Miriam Williams."

"Miss Williams was released a few weeks ago," he states. They have hung up as it goes dead.

Okay, now I know Miriam has gone. I need to find where she went. How the heck am I going to do that?

CHAPTER SIX

-:- MIA -:-

The last four weeks, we've thankfully not had a single MC member in the diner. I hope they've decided to eat somewhere else.

Being here with Graham and Suzie is great; they treat me like family, and it's the first time in years anyone has treated me like that. Even before Gunner, being brought up in foster homes was never easy, and getting my education and a job in the bank was something I could be very proud of, then I lost it all.

Shaking myself out of this pity party, I finish cleaning my apartment and then get ready to walk into town, look for some new shoes, and, depending on how much, a new pair of jeans.

Reaching the bottom of the stairs, I hear Suzie in the diner talking to someone, and when I hear, "Oh, Mia's not at work today." I stop and listen.

"What days does she work?" a man asks, I can't see who it is without being seen myself, so I hang back and then notice Graham waving his hand behind his back at me to move away.

Carefully I turn and tiptoe back up the stairs to my apartment. Shit, this is not good and could be the start of me having to pack up and move on. I hoped for longer, but it seems as though my time here's run out.

A while later, a soft tapping on my door catches my attention, and I walk over and open it slightly, keeping the chain on just in case.

Seeing Suzie standing there, I take the chain off and open the door. She rushes in and shuts the door behind her.

"It was that MC asking about you, the one I said kept looking at you. Not the one that you're running from. I told him you were off for the day and out and about somewhere. He didn't ask more, but I noticed he kept looking at the kitchen, probably to see if you came back." she sits down heavily at the kitchen table and rests her head in her hands.

"I'm sorry, Suzie. This is not good for you. I'm going to pack up and move on. I'll be out by the end of the week." I feel like crying, but I am not going to allow myself that luxury. I haven't cried in five years, and I'm not going to start now.

"We don't want you to move on, Mia. We want you to stay with us, you're like a daughter to us, and if we could adopt you, we would." Suzie states and a single tear rolls down her cheek.

"I won't put you in danger. I couldn't live with that. If this MC is starting to become aware of who I could be, then it won't be long before the other one does, and then we could be in danger. They could burn this place down, hurt you both. No, I won't have that happen, Suzie. I care about you both too much." hugging Suzie as I know I'll have to sneak away, or they won't let me go.

"We'll talk about this tomorrow with Graham, don't do anything stupid, Mia, don't run, at least until we've spoken to you about this." and she takes my hand into hers, squeezing it gently. I nod, but I'm not even sure how honest I'm being right now.

Once Suzie has left, I walk into the bedroom and find my backpack. Checking through my clothes, I select the ones I'll need most: jeans, t-shirts, and a sweater.

I place the money I've saved into a large envelope. I tuck it into the torn lining of the pack. I'm leaving a small amount in my wallet for me to use for bus fare. Placing a few essentials onto the top of the bag, shampoo, conditioner, body wash, toothpaste, toothbrush, plus a hairbrush. I have everything I'm going to need for basics.

Laying on top of the bed, I know I'll have to get a few hours' sleep as I don't know when I'll next be able to close my eyes. I know what it's like to sleep with one eye open, it's no fun, but we do what we have to do to stay alive.

Memories of being locked up flash through my mind, my hair being pulled hard as someone tries to get a toothbrush ground down, so it's a blade to my throat. Punches in my back as I walk past people, spitting into my food as they walk past the dining table where I was sitting.

I shake my head and stop the images and memories. Making a new life is my priority and leaving all this in the past. To do that, I have to shake off the bad that hangs over my head.

-:- CRACK -:-

After catching Cara treating Zara like that, I drag her out to the office and throw her down in front of Sharp, our President; her wailing and screaming are just making me want to shut her up for good.

"What's goin' on, Crack?" he asks, looking at me and then down at this fucking bitch.

"Caught this bitch mistreating Zara, throwing her on the floor in the kitchen." I spit out, feeling like kicking the fucker while she's down.

"What the fuck!" Sharp snaps, shooting a look at Cara.

"Funny thing is Pres, Zara tried to hide behind me when she saw this bitch. She was scared of her, so what the fuck has she been doing to her?" I snarl, "Where the fuck is Gunner these days, he told me he hadn't seen Zara in days."

"He doesn't care about anyone, only himself." Cara snaps as she stands and throws her hands onto her hips.

"Are you fuckin' surprised? You had the love of his life thrown in prison for something she didn't do and don't think for a fuckin' minute I don't know what you did." stepping right into her, which has her back-peddling fast, or I would have knocked her over.

"I didn't do nothin'. She stabbed me." shouting, spittle flying as she does.

Stepping forward, I wrap my hand around her neck and start to squeeze. It wouldn't take anything for me to kill this bitch.

"Let go of her Crack," Sharp snarls as he jumps up from his desk. Opening his cell, I hear him snarl, "Bring Gunner to my office now."

I let go of her, alright. I throw her back onto the floor just as she did to Zara.

Sharp walks over to the front of his desk, staring down at the bitch, "Where's Zara?"

"I don't know. He dragged me in here." she spouts off, pointing at me with attitude. I'm about done with this bitch and itching to give her a bullet.

Gunner walks into the office and sees Cara on the floor, "What the fuck is goin' on?"

"This bitch was mistreating Zara, caught her myself, she threw Zara on the fuckin' floor in the kitchen." making sure I stayed near this bitch, ready to take her out, if necessary, I never hated a woman, but I hate this one.

"Where's Zara Gunner?" Pres asks, and I can tell by his face he knows that the answer is not going to be good.

"No idea Pres," Gunner responds, then looks down at Cara, "Where is she?"

"I don't know. The little bitch ran off after he grabbed me." She mouths off.

"You find her, and you find her now," he shouts.

"What you shouting at her for? She's your daughter too. You admit you've not seen her for days. This bitch has been mistreating her, and how do I know? Because Zara was hiding behind me to stay away from this bitch." I shout right in Gunner's face. I'm enraged and about ready to pop them both off.

"You two, go find your daughter and bring her to me." Sharp snarls, dragging Cara up off the floor and throwing her at Gunner.

When they've both left the office, I slam the door and turn to Sharp. "Something is terribly wrong, Zara is nearly thirteen, and she's scared of her mother. Her father doesn't give a damn, the same father who was supposed to be so enraged when Miriam stabbed Cara because of jealousy over Zara. Now, why would Miriam stab Cara unless she was protecting Zara? That is how I see it."

"I agree, Crack, and I want you to start digging, find out what happened, why Zara has never spoken since it happened either." Sharp sits behind his desk and runs his hands over the paperwork in front of him, "I was to blame at that time too. I had so much work that I struggled to find time to sleep. I allowed Miriam to be railroaded. I'll always regret it as she was good for the MC. She helped everyone, and all of us should have stood up to find out what went on."

Nodding agreement, "I'll see what I can find out, it's five years too late, but I'll try and get Zara to talk to me."

"With Miriam being Gunner's ol' lady, we had the issue where he got the last word, and that's what happened. He shut it all down, stopped anyone from getting near her. He could do that again if he finds out you're digging around, so keep it on the down-low the best you can." Sharp states, nodding at the door for me to leave, then adds, "Crack, I'll override him this time if I need to."

Walking out of Sharp's office, I keep my eyes peeled as to who's watching. Also, I need to find Zara and why she is frightened, and what she has to say about what happened with Miriam back then.

-:- ZARA -:-

Rushing back to my hiding place, I quickly climb up and put the hatch down. I'm going to find Miriam, I know what town she was in, and I'm taking my savings and going to find her. I don't want to be here anymore. It's not safe.

Cara hates me, and I hate her. My dad, I love, but he doesn't care anymore, not since Miriam was sent to prison. I've seen him going into bedrooms with the club women. I know he sleeps around with all of them. Well, he can have them as I'm going to make a run for it.

Making sure I have the laptop, cell, and savings, I tuck them into the backpack I stole out of my dad's closet. He won't know as he's never home.

Looking at the time, I know I have to wait until everyone goes to bed before I can sneak out. There's a break in the fencing at the back of the compound, I've been through it before, so I know where to get out. I have to make sure one of the prospects doesn't catch me.

"Zara, where are you?"

Oh no, that's my dad looking for me. I crawl near the hatch and place my ear on it. I'm not going to open it.

"Zara, where are you? Come out now."

I hear my dad shouting, but he has Cara with him. I can hear her bitching about what a worthless little bitch I am.

When I grow up, I'm gonna learn how to shoot and fight. I'm not having someone like her calling me names. I need to find Miriam. She loved me, and she protects me.

When the clubhouse is quiet, I check the cellphone and see it's three in the morning. I'm going to make my move and get out of here. I need to walk to the bus station and find the one that takes me to the town where the prison is to look for Miriam.

Slipping out of the loft, I grab the backpack and quietly make my way out of the clubhouse, dodging someone as they make their way towards the bedrooms.

As I pass the main room, I hear my dad talking to someone, telling them he can't find me and he'll look again tomorrow. Good luck with that, I think to myself.

I squeeze out the back door, trying not to let any light out that will have the prospect looking this way. I know one is on the gate, and one walks around the edges of the fencing, so I have to get out when they've walked away.

Creeping to the picnic table, I duck behind it and wait until the prospect passes, then I dash to the fence and squeeze out. I keep low as I don't want to be seen, but I take off running once I get a little way away. I want to get to town as fast as possible, then I can get the first bus, so I keep running for as long as I can before I run out of breath and start gasping.

When I get to where I have to walk up the side of the road, I keep watch, and every time a vehicle comes, I duck behind anything I can so I'm not seen.

It's a bit frightening as it's still dark and I can hear animals moving around. But I'm not stopping. I need to get away before they find I'm missing.

CHAPTER SEVEN

-:- AXEL -:-

Walking into the clubhouse kitchen, I can't believe the fucking mess that has been left in here. I wash a cup and pour a coffee from the machine, I'm not sure how long ago it was made, but it's hot at least.

I steadily walk through the main room, looking around at the state of everything. This is going to be sorted this morning.

Opening the Church door, I walk to my seat at the table. The logo of the club is painted on the wall behind me. I've always been proud and still am, but the brothers have got to up their game.

Leaning back, I patiently wait for everyone to settle into their seats. It takes about twenty minutes before everyone is here and seated.

Drag leans over to me, "Women all in the office, and Jig is watching them."

Giving him a nod, I pick up my gavel and hit the table, "Okay, meeting open, I'm not fuckin' around with it this morning. How many of you have done any kind of cleaning in the last few months?"

The faces on them would be fucking funny if I didn't feel like I was about to blow my fuse.

"Okay, let's go around the fucking room then, Knuckle. When did you last pick up any trash?"

He looks at me as if I'm joking.

"So, by the looks of you, not any time in the recent past. You Brag, when did you last pick up anything?"

Brag sits straighter, "I cleaned all the kitchen out last Friday, the fridge had moldy shit in it, and I emptied it all, then sent prospect Brad to get a load of stuff from the store."

Nodding at him, letting him know I appreciate it.

"Silver, you?" I add. He nods, shaking his head no.

"So, let's shorten this, shall we?" I snarl, leaning forward over the table, "The place looks like shit, the place stinks like shit, you need to get out of the shit place you're living. We didn't work our asses off to get this place and the businesses up and running to let it slide like this." This has a few sitting up and grumbling. Still, I don't give a fuck how they feel about it, "The women are loose pussy who are living off our backs. They are doing fuck all to clean up, cook, or anything else. They cost us thousands every year." I stand to let them know how angry I am about all this, and I lean over the table, placing my knuckles on the wood and give everyone the eye.

"What do you want us to do, Pres?" Rock asks, and I know he is not being a prick as he is a good brother who does anything I ask whenever I ask.

"We have to make a decision today, now, do we boot out the women or do they stay and earn their keep. They need to cook and clean at a minimum. It would cost less to pay a cleaning company to come in." I state and maintain my anger, so they all know I've had it with this bullshit.

For the next hour, we discuss what will happen in the future, how we move forward with keeping the place clean, and if we keep the club women around.

"Okay, let's vote on the women, do they stay?" and ayes apart from two who say nay, majority rules, so they stay.

"So, they stay, do they earn their keep by cooking and cleaning?" I ask, again, ayes go around and this time unanimous.

"Who will volunteer to oversee this gets done?" I lean back in my chair and wait. After a minute, Hammer speaks up, "I'll do it, Pres, but I need someone to do it with me. As you know, I can't always be here."

Brag states he'll help Hammer and keep the women in line or boot them out if needed. We all agree that we'll leave this to them to deal with, and if they need help to come back to me.

"Okay, everyone, clean your room. Let's all help get the place in order. Then the women can keep it that way." I look around once more, and they are all in agreement, so I hit the gavel and close the meeting.

"Drag, Buzz, and Specs stay behind," I state firmly, stepping up and closing the door behind the brothers.

"What's up, Pres?" Drag asks, sitting again and leaning on the table with his forearms.

" Specs, what have you found out so far about the woman from the diner?" I ask as I'm sure now it's the same woman who went to prison, just my gut instinct shouting at me.

"The information I received from my source shows she didn't have it easy in prison to start with. She had to defend herself numerous times. Inside she was called Blade because she fashioned something to use as a blade to keep herself safe. She did a lot of time on her own, not making friends or even talking to anyone. From what I understand, the MC put out an order that her life be as hard as they could make it without killing her." Specs informs us, and I'm not surprised somehow.

Placing an image on the table of the woman in her prison garb when she was sent down and one of the women in the diner has far too many similarities not to be the same person.

The hair color is wrong, but dye will do that. The eye color is not correct, but contacts will sort that. But as I'd seen before, her mouth, cheeks, and eye shape are the same. If you place one image over the other, it shows the same person.

"It's the same person," Drag says and blows out a breath he must have been holding.

"I think so," Specs states. He brings up more information, "I printed off all I could find from newspaper reports at the time and the court transcripts. I think you were right, Pres, she was railroaded, now by who and for what reason I don't know." he continues, "Miriam had been the ol' lady of Gunner for five years, brought the kid up from 2 years of age. The odd thing is that not one single word has been recorded from Miriam."

"Okay," I run my hands down the back of my neck, "Buzz take Mav and pick her up as soon as you get the chance. Bring her back here. I don't want her hurt at all. I just want to know what happened and who railroaded her."

"Why Pres?" Buzz asks me, looking at me intently, "What does it matter to us?"

"It doesn't, but I don't like it. I have that itchy feeling, and I just gotta know what the fuck happened and if she did do it. My gut tells me no. Suppose I'm just fuckin' nosy." I state and then walk out of Church and head for my office.

-:- MIA -:-

It's time to move. I pick up my backpack and look around at the apartment, where I have found a small amount of peace. Now it's time to move and get far from here while I can.

I leave a note on the counter in the kitchen for Suzie to find and leave locking up the diner's back door and sliding the key under.

Thankfully it's still dark, and I can move before the town starts to wake and people see me walking around town. I need to get to the bus station, and on the first one out of here, it doesn't matter where as long as it takes me away from here.

Walking along the side of the road, I keep looking at the tree line on my right. I'm sure I keep hearing an animal moving around. Nerves start to grind, and I take my blade from the holder on my calf. Squeezing the handle gives me a feeling of being in control, and I start taking calming breaths as I walk, listening for any movement.

Hearing bikes gets my attention, and when I see headlights coming towards me, I quickly jump into the tree line and place my back to a sturdy tree but turn my head so I can watch them pass.

As soon as they've passed, I get back on the road and power walk to cover as much ground as I can. I may need to run, so I want to keep some energy for that if it's needed.

On the edge of town, it's light enough now that I'm not going to be able to hide anymore. I make it to the bus station and have half an hour to stay out of the way before the first bus leaves.

Picking up a couple of bottles of water, chips, and a newspaper, I sit in the food court, tapping on the table as nerves start to get the better of me.

I keep looking at the clock to see how much longer I have to wait, and with only ten minutes to go, I head for the bus, which now has passengers boarding.

Climbing on, I place myself midway down and sit with my back to the window, hoping no one knows me from the diner. I hear bikes, and looking around, I see two slowing, coming up alongside the bus, so I quickly slide down in my seat and pull the hood up on my hoodie.

A woman pushes me down further, sits next to me, and throws her jacket over me as well as a couple of bags, "Stay down; they won't see with those on top. Keep still and quiet."

I hear boots stomping along the bus aisle, and the woman sitting here has taken her cell out as she is talking to someone or pretending to talk to someone.

The steps stop, and I can see a pair of biker boots next to the woman's foot. I hold my breath with fear, but I'll fight if I have to.

"You see a woman with long black hair? About five-four in height?" the biker asks the woman. He also is checking out the area, trying to see if he can find me.

"Nope," the woman fidgets, "Can you not see I'm speaking to someone?" she's good at acting, sounds put out, and if I wasn't in this mess, I would laugh at her antics. She would earn a lot of green if she took it up professionally.

The biker stomps off, and the woman pats my arm. As the bus sets off, she taps me again, "Okay, they've driven off, and we're on our way." She gives me a huge smile and a wink.

I sit up next to the woman, look over at her, "Thank you so much, that was kind of you."

"Don't care who you are, my lovely, but I know men, and no way was I letting bikers find you, not on my watch," she states, grinning broadly at me.

I hold out my hand, "I'm Mia."

"I'm Chrissie. Nice to meet you girl," she responds, grinning again.

We spent the next two hours of the journey talking about everything and nothing. She lets me know she is going to live with her cousin as she dumped her *no-good husband,* as she calls him.

I tell her about coming out of prison, leaving the diner to get away, and that I didn't do anything but protect the child, and she believed me, only the third person to hear my story and believe me. It made me feel good.

Chrissie gives me her cellphone number on a scrap of paper, and I tuck it into my backpack, I doubt I will ever use it, but it was nice of her to care enough to give it to me.

At the end of the journey, we are in Rainsville, still in Nevada. The town is small, and I'll just stay one night then catch another bus somewhere even farther away. Once I've done this a few times, I'll see if I can disappear to a place off the beaten track and make a life. For now, keep moving.

CHAPTER EIGHT

-:- CRACK -:-

Walking through the kitchen, I see Gunner, Cara, and a couple of others sitting drinking coffee. I can't stand to be near Cara. She's an evil bitch, and I will never understand why people don't see that in her.

"Has Zara been found yet?" I ask as I lean on the door frame that leads into the dining area.

"No, not a sign. I've looked everywhere." Gunner snarls, by the look of him, he's been up all night, yet Cara looks fresh.

"You been up all night?" tipping the rest of the coffee in the sink as it taste's like shit.

"Yeah, I've searched everywhere." Gunner runs his hands over his face, looking pretty defeated.

"What about you, Cara? Where have you looked?" I know the fucking answer before I ask, but I want to open the eyes of anyone I can that she is a heartless bitch.

She doesn't even bother to answer, just shrugs her shoulders and carries on drinking her coffee.

"So, your daughter is missing, and all you can do is shrug, not caring a fuck what's happened to her?" I snarl.

"Gunner's been looking for her." Cara eventually says but still looks like she doesn't give a damn.

"And you threw Miriam under the bus for this bitch Gunner? Take a good look at her brother. She's the guilty one in all that shit. Have you never asked yourself why Zara has never spoken a single word since it happened? Why does she hide from her so-called mother?" I say, getting more aggressive as I speak.

Gunner turns more to look at me, then curls his lip, "She doesn't speak 'cause she's traumatized, and we all know who did that to her."

"Do we? You never allowed anyone to speak to Miriam. You even paid the cops to railroad Miriam. You took it even farther and had her life made hell in prison. All while this piece of shit sits here smirking. I'll find out the truth, Cara, and when I do, you're a dead woman." I snarl, then as I'm walking out, I turn, "And you Gunner, you'll get the beating you deserve."

Jumping up, Gunner comes at me, but before he reaches where I'm standing, and I have to add I'm fucking waiting, Sharp walks into the kitchen, "Stand down, Gunner," and then turns to me, "You're right Crack, we need to find out what the fuck happened, and Gunner you're not getting involved this time."

Nodding, "I'm gonna look for Zara. She's been missing for hours. If she's not in the compound, I'm goin' outside to find her. All of us here need to be lookin'. Something's not right with her and hasn't been for a long time. She's been seen less and less, and has anyone noticed at all that she's not been at meals for weeks?"

I make sure my disgust is aimed at Gunner and Cara as they are responsible for Zara and are failing her daily.

As I leave the kitchen, I hear Sharp speaking to Trip, our VP, "Make sure Cara doesn't leave the compound, even if you need to lock her ass up, and Gunner, you make any complaint, and you can fucking join her." nothing can stop the broad smirk that crosses my face.

-:- ZARA -:-

It feels like it was a long way walking to town, but I've made it at last. I'm going to get a ticket for the bus and hope no one asks me any questions.

The Greyhound bus is waiting to leave, and I tell the woman I'm buying the ticket to see my grandmother. I'm not sure if she believes me, but she gives me the ticket.

The bus will take me near the prison, still in Nevada, but about six towns away, I think, looking at the map I purchased.

I sit near the back of the bus and place my backpack on the seat next to me, taking out a bag of chips and a bottle of water. I'm tired, but I can't go to sleep.

Arriving at our destination, I look around the bus terminal and chew my lip as I don't know which way to go from here. Seeing a man sitting on the floor at the side of the hallway, I walk over to ask if he can help me.

"Excuse me," I say quietly, "Could you tell me which way I need to go to find the prison, please?"

"Why girlie? Why do you want to go there?" he says.

"I'm trying to find my friend who just got out of prison. I need to find her," I tell him and sit down next to him as I'm tired.

"I can tell you where the prison is, but if she is out now, then you won't get any information from them. She would have gone by bus to the halfway house, then wherever she wants from that place." he tells me, "Are you on your own?"

"Oh," I don't know what to do now, "Can you tell me where to go to ask?"

"I tell you what, I'll go with, and make sure nobody bothers you," he states and gives me a small smile.

Should I trust him? I need help, that is for sure. I hold my hand out to shake his, "My name is Zara."

"Hi Zara, my name is Peter." we shake hands, and he stands.

I follow Peter, and he asks if I'm okay, if someone hurt me. Looking at Peter, I don't know why but I know I can trust him even though he needs a bath. He's about six-three, I cannot see how fit he is as he has a lot of old clothes on, but he has dark hair and eyes that have a twinkle in them.

We talk as we journey to the halfway house, and he tells me he was a Green Beret, left when he lost most of his team and that he's not sure what he wants to do now. I tell him why I'm looking for Miriam and about my parents. He seems pretty pissed when I tell him Cara hits me.

Finally, we get to the halfway house, and we go inside. It's dark here, a bit miserable looking, and needs decorating. At the back of the room, I see a woman sitting behind a desk.

Walking over, I stand before the desk, smiling at the lady. "Hello, I'm looking for a lady called Miriam Williams. She left prison and came here. I need to find her."

"Why do you need to find her?" the woman asks, looking past me at Peter.

"She's my friend, and I need to find her," I tell the woman. "She didn't do what they said she did, and I want to tell her I'm sorry that I didn't get a chance to tell anyone."

"Oh, well, let me have a look for you."

I look behind me to see Peter standing near the door, watching what is happening, and I give him a small smile.

"Okay, she got a job at a diner just outside of town. Here's the address. Do you need help? Apart from finding her?" she asks me.

"No, thank you, my friend Peter is helping me." and I take the paper that she wrote down the address, and I walk back over to Peter.

We leave the building, and Peter points to a park across the road. We find a bench and sit. I take out a couple of my protein bars and give one to Peter, plus a bottle of water, and we sit quietly while we eat and drink.

Peter turns to me, "Do you want to go to the diner, see if she's still there?"

"Yes," I murmur but start to lean on Peter as I'm trying hard to keep my eyes open.

"Okay, little girl, we'll go to the diner when you've had a nap; put your head on my lap and close your eyes a while," he says, but before he's finished speaking, I'm already asleep.

-:- AXEL -:-

After the meeting in Church, everyone seems a bit more understanding about the state the place has gotten into, and I'm pleased to see that the women have been told to shape up or ship out, and I don't care either way.

Specs calls to me, and I walk over to him where he's standing in his office doorway.

"What's up, Specs?"

"I've heard back from a friend who owed me one," said with a half-grin, "He talked to a guard he knows and got some information."

In his office, he closes the door, and I take a seat. Specs grabs a notepad off his desk and hands it to me. Reading the information has my blood boiling with anger. The MC that was supposed to be her family had her more than railroaded; they wanted her dead, well, her old man did.

Looking up at Specs, the look on his face must mirror mine, outrage, disbelief, and anger. I turn the page and continue reading.

This woman was not allowed to speak to anyone, not from her MC, the lawyer she had, or the court. She was allowed no opportunity to defend herself.

Then inside, she was targeted by women who were paid to make her life miserable and kill her if they had the chance. Even guards were paid to look the other way.

The report shows medical visits she had due to a stab wound in her side. Hair ripped out, leaving a bleeding scalp, multiple black eyes, and twice broken ribs.

I don't like any of this; our club helps women in distress when we get the opportunity. We don't have a business set up for it as some MCs, but we do what we can if it ever comes onto our radar. This has to be the worst case of betrayal I've ever seen.

Turning to Specs, "Where the fuck is Buzz and Mav? They should be back by now with the woman."

"Not heard anything Pres, do you want me to try to find them?" he asks as he picks his cell up from the desk.

"Na, I'll do it. You carry on, and thanks, Specs." I say as I leave him to it. I call Buzz and wait for his answer.

"Yoh, Pres."

"Buzz, where the fuck are you?" I snap out.

"We're checking all the buses that left. We missed her at the diner. She has to have been on one of the two that left before the diner opened, and we spoke to the couple that owns the place," he sighs, "Pres, they were pissed she's run, they said she served time for something she didn't do, and we should leave her the fuck alone."

"Find her. You should be able to catch up with her, but if you need to call in more brothers, do it. I want her found and brought here," I state firmly.

Entering my office, I decide to contact Sharp over at Rogue Legion MC. I've had dealings with him in the past and found him to be fair, a bit rough around the edges, but then aren't we all?

The call is answered after five rings, "Who's this?" the gruff voice snarls.

"Sharp, this is Axel from Raging Barons MC. I want to ask you a couple of questions if that's okay. If not, that's okay too, as I'll get my answers one way or another," I state calmly.

"Axel, what can I do for you?" Sharp more calmly asks.

"I'm looking into something that involved your MC a few years back and wondered if you could give me a couple of answers to something that's bugging me." Keeping it cool at this point as I don't want this fucker to take offense, but if he does, fuck him.

"Okay, Axel, what's your questions?"

"You had a young woman sent to prison for something she didn't do. Can you tell me the reason behind that? If you have a good reason, then I'll back off, but otherwise, I want to know what actually happened, you know, what happened, not the bullshit that was spouted." I have a grin on my face that he obviously can't see, but Sting, one of my brothers, can see as he just walked into my office.

Sting is a brother that will do anything asked of him, but he is damn good at torturing if needed. He was an exceptional prospect and was patched in early as no one thought he would be anything but an excellent brother. He's six-one, brown hair with flecks of red, green eyes, and well built.

"We're just looking into it ourselves, Axel. Something's just not ringing true at our end either. Things were crazy at the time, and I didn't look into it as I should have, just let it slide past me. I know things are not adding up," Sharp inhales hard, "I didn't know she was railroaded, and still not for sure, but one of my men is convinced she was set up by her ol' man's baby mama. The trouble is, the baby is now twelve, nearly thirteen, and she's gone missing. I have a feeling she's gone to find Miriam. Zara has not spoken one word to any of us since the day it happened. We all thought it was trauma; now, I'm not so sure of that either."

"I've got my boys looking for Miriam; as I said, I want to know what happened, and if all the people that were paid off knowing that she was innocent, then I'm gonna be doing some damage. We don't help women just to sit back and watch this injustice stand. You got me, Sharp?" I say with the hardest edge I can to my voice, this whole thing has a bad stink about it and I'm determined to get to the bottom of it.

"Keep me updated, Axel, and I'll let you know if we find Zara or Miriam," Sharp responds, before ending the call.

Taking a deep breath, I sit back down and get down to business with Sting even though my mind keeps wandering.

CHAPTER NINE

-:- MIA -:-

Leaving the motel, I make sure I look around for any bikers. I need to stay alert as I don't know who is looking for me or why. But I can guess it's for nothing good.

Walking to the bus depot, I'm thinking what a great day it's going to be, the sun is starting to warm, the air smells fresh and although I've no idea where I'm going, I'm glad to be alive.

Purchasing my next Greyhound ticket, I get settled and check out the scenery as we travel. I hopefully will get out of Nevada tomorrow and into Utah. From that point, I'm not sure which way to head.

Hearing bikes, I lower myself into my seat and watch out the window as four bikers pass with an SUV keeping pace. I couldn't see the kutte they were wearing, but I'm avoiding every MC I can. I want nothing to do with any of them.

The bus journey ends at the border of Nevada meeting Utah. I head for a bed and breakfast across from the bus depot. I'm tired, I need food and a hot shower, then lots of sleep.

Knocking on the door to the bed and breakfast, an older lady answers, "Hello, I'm looking for a night's stay if you have a vacancy?" I quickly ask her.

"One night?" she smiles, "Come on in, we can do one night, honey."

The room she shows me is small but clean, and I'm happy to pay her the amount she asks me for. We arranged that I could have breakfast early so I can get the first Greyhound in the morning.

I pay her, and she gives me a key to the room. Once she's left, I jump straight into the shower and let the hot water run over my body, easing some of the aches caused by sitting so long.

Once dried, I wear the pj's I had brought with me, then settle on the bed. Picking up my cell, I ring Suzie. It only takes four rings before she picks up.

"Mia, are you alright? Why did you run off like that?" Suzie quickly says, and I can tell she's upset by her voice.

"I'm sorry, Suzie, but I couldn't put you in any danger. I care about you too much. You and Graham have been so good to me." I say, resting back against the headboard.

"Two men came looking for you. From one of those biker clubs. I forgot to look which one, but I told them you didn't do anything wrong and went to prison for someone else's evil deed," Suzie spits out, "I told them I don't know where you are and basically to fuck off." which has her giggling as she's never one to swear.

"Oh, Suzie, you're so bad swearing." I smile, although she can't see it.

"I know, but I don't care. I'm not going to ask where you are but are you safe? For now, at least." she asks.

"Yes, for now, I'm safe. I'm at a bed and breakfast for the night. Then I'll move farther away again tomorrow." I can tell her that much.

"Keep in touch with me every few days, Mia, please."

"Yes, I'll contact you again, Suzie. Take care of you both, stay safe." and I end the call, putting my head back and taking a deep breath.

The next day I'm up early, eat some toast and scrambled eggs for breakfast, and head over to the depot to get on the first bus out.

As I reach the depot, someone grabs me from behind, slams a hand over my mouth, and I feel a sharp stab in my neck. That's when I realize I'm in real trouble as the dizziness and the spots start before my eyes. I've been drugged, and everything goes black.

-:- CRACK -:-

Zara is nowhere in sight. I've searched every inch of the clubhouse and compound. She has to have left, but where would she go and why would she leave.

Re-entering the clubhouse, I make my way to Sharp's office and knock, waiting to be called to enter. Sharp hates anyone just walking in as he could be on the telephone or discussing something private.

"Come in," I enter the office and see Sharp behind his desk, looking over what looks like the accounts book.

"Pres, I can't find Zara anywhere in the clubhouse or at the compound. Can I get a couple of guys to go with me to check out the town, see if we can find where she is?" I ask, pacing somewhat as I have a bad feeling about where she may be.

"Take Runner, Tin, and Glue with you. Keep me informed. Oh, take fucking Gunner with you, let's make him do something worthwhile, shall we?" and Sharp has a nasty smile on his face, one we don't see very often.

"Will do, with pleasure," I state, turn and leave the office and walk into the main room but don't see Gunner anywhere.

"Runner, Tin, Glue with me. Has anyone seen Gunner?" I shout.

Trip points to the kitchen, and I head that way. Opening the kitchen door, I could punch Gunner. He's sitting at the kitchen table with a whore going down on him while he eats his fucking breakfast.

Reaching over, I grab her by the hair and throw her to the side, turning to sneer at Gunner. "You're here having that bitch go down on you while your daughter is missing. Get your fucking gear NOW. We're on our way to look for her, Sharps orders." and I don't fucking wait for him to come or respond. I head outside to my bike, making sure the three I called in the main room are with me.

Throwing my leg over my bike, I slam my helmet on and start her up. Not waiting for anyone else, I take off, giving a slight nod to the prospect on the gate as I pass.

By the time we reach the town, Gunner's caught up, but I've had it with him; he can fuck right off for all I care.

Once I pull over, I turn and face the others, "Tin, Runner, you both head to the other side of town. Glue and I will start this side. We'll meet at the diner in the middle of town."

Gunner mumbles something under his breath, but I don't wait to hear. Pulling out, I slowly cruise around the streets, watching for a sign of Zara.

When we meet up at the diner, no sign of Zara, my gut tells me bad things, but I don't want to voice anything. "Glue, go back to the clubhouse, tell Sharp no sign, and I'm gonna see what buses have left in the last 48hrs. Maybe we need to see if she left town."

"Okay, Crack," starting his bike back up, he takes off.

Gunner steps over to me. Now he's looking worried, "What do you think, Crack?"

"I think she left town." pulling my helmet back on.

"Fuck, why would she leave?" Gunner asks, and I just give him a look that I don't think he can even decipher.

Pulling away, I head for the bus depot. Once we've parked up, I turn to the others, "Ask everyone you can if they've seen her, don't leave anyone out."

An hour later, we've met back up at our bikes, "Anyone heard anything?" Gunner asks, now he is worried, and I have no sympathy.

No one has any news, except I do, and now I have to tell them, "Well, I have news," I turn to Gunner, "A girl meeting Zara's description left yesterday morning on a Greyhound, stating she was going to her grandmothers. The route for that bus is to the same town where we ate at that diner."

Looking right at Gunner, "The same town the correctional facility is where Miriam was held until a few months ago." Gunner looks up at me. Now he is beginning to understand.

"Fuck, we've got to find her." Gunner snarls, running his hands around the back of his neck.

"Yeah, and why would Zara run to Miriam if Miriam had hurt her? Ask yourself that fucker." I snarl back at him.

Glue arrives back with us, and we set off even though it's getting late in the day. We don't have time to waste with Zara on her own in a strange place; anything could happen to her.

Runner calls and updates Sharp on where we're going and that we'll keep him updated regularly. He catches up with us a short way into the journey.

CHAPTER TEN

-:- ZARA -:-

Waking up in the park, I don't know how long we've been sleeping. Sitting up, I wake Peter and tell him we need to eat; I'm hungry now.

"Peter, you need to wake up now," I say gently.

"I'm awake. Are you okay?" he asks, rubbing his hands over his eyes.

"Yes, but I'm hungry. Let's go find something to eat." I say, standing and putting my backpack on.

"Don't have any money, Zara. We can find something in a trash can behind the drive-through, I have money in an account, but we would need to go to the bank," he tells me. Oh yuck, that's not happening. I'm not eating out the trash.

"No, Peter, we're going to have some dinner, come on, I've got some money, I can buy us dinner. You need to tell me where we're going to sleep tonight." I don't wait for him to argue as I start walking out of the park, looking at the shops for somewhere we can buy food.

"Zara, come with me if you have some money, we can buy some food from the food cart as it's cheaper and good." and as he turns to walk the other way, I follow, no idea where I am, but somehow, I trust Peter. As we're walking, I slide my hand into Peter's, and he looks down at me, then smiles, and I smile back.

The food cart smells great, the man serving smiles and says hello to Peter, and we order large burgers, fries, and onion rings. As we walk away, I run back and get us a can of soda each, and the man serving only takes the money from me for one, to which I give him my biggest smile.

We sit on the grass in front of someone's house and eat quickly. We were both starving. After we've had our drinks, we make sure we take our cans and used napkins to the garbage bin at the side of the food cart and walk away.

"Peter, where are we going to sleep tonight? I need the toilet." I say, looking up at him.

"You're coming with me. I'll make sure you're safe. We're going where I sleep most nights." he tells me, and I follow wherever he is taking me.

A couple of streets away, Peter goes into a house and leads me to the bathroom, telling me not to take too long as it's going to get dark soon.

Once I've washed my hands, I find Peter, and he has a pile of blankets on the floor and nods to get on them. As I get settled, Peter closes the door and wedges it closed with a wooden block and a chair, now no one can get in.

"Why do you live here?" I ask him, surprised he doesn't have a real home.

"I was in the military as I told you, and when I'd served my time, I didn't know where to go or what to do. So, I just bummed around a bit, and now I'm still bumming around," he tells me.

"When I find Miriam, I want her to come home with me, but I want you to come home with me too, Peter," I tell him.

"I can't go home with you," he tells me, looking at me as though I'm a bit odd.

"Yes, you can. You can come home and be a prospect. Then when you do a year, you can be a full brother." I tell him, I know that as I've seen them being patched in.

Peter is studying my face, not sure what he is seeing as it's getting a bit darker now. "Do you come from a home of bikers? A motorcycle club?"

"Yes, you'll love it, Peter, you can be a brother too," I tell him excitedly. "Do you have a different name, Peter? My dad's called Gunner, and our Pres is Sharp. We have Crack, Trip, Zip, and others."

Peter studies me again for a minute, "I was called Target, 'cause I never missed my target." he rubs his hand over his face and neck, "My unit of brothers all died, except one, and I was injured but survived. I couldn't do it anymore, not without my team, so I left."

"That's sad. I'm sorry you lost your friends. You can make new friends when you come with me. I'm going to call you Target so you know I'm your friend, your sister, I can't be a brother as I'm not a boy." and I giggle, then wrap my arms around Target, look up and say, "Thank you for looking after me."

"You're welcome. I'll watch and make sure you're safe. We need to find your friend as soon as we can." Target tells me, "Now, let's get to sleep."

-:- MIA -:-

Turning my head, a headache hits me. Lifting my hand, I rub my forehead and slowly crack my eyes open. As soon as my vision clears, I start to panic. Where the fuck am I?

Looking around the room, I'm in a bedroom, not one I recognize. I slowly pull myself into a sitting position and twist so my legs are off the bed.

Once again, rubbing my forehead as this headache is pounding, then I remember someone grabbing me, placing a hand over my mouth, and the pinch in my neck. Some fucker drugged me, I realize.

Someone's taken my shoes off. Where are they? I need to get the fuck out of here before they come back. Seeing my shoes next to a chair under the window, I grab them, then I start to slip them on, holding the window sill as I do, and that's when I look out and see men in kuttes.

Panic hits. Who the fuck are they? This is not Gunner's MC as I don't recognize the place, so why would another MC grab me? Well, I'm not waiting around to find out.

Searching around, I see my backpack and rush over and pick it up, then walk to the door and turn the handle, which thankfully opens. What I didn't want to find was a man sitting opposite my door on guard.

He looks over and takes out a cell, obviously to report to someone that I'm awake. While he's texting, I make a run for it down the hall, lunging at the door at the end and thankfully finding a set of stairs. I take the stairs as fast as I can because I still feel a little dizzy, and the headache is worse now I'm getting worked up.

I can hear the man behind me but don't slow to see how close he is to me. He keeps calling for me to stop. At the bottom of the stairs, I run down a hallway and into a large room where twenty men must be sitting around.

As I start to run through, one of the men jumps up and stands in front of me. The man who had been sitting across from my room is telling me to calm down.

More men start to stand until they've blocked my path to what I think is the main door to the outside. Taking a deep breath, I drop my backpack and bend, taking my blade that's strapped to my calf, and stand waiting, twisting now and again to check no one is coming up behind me.

I quickly decide I need my back to the wall, so I step back gently until I'm positioned with a wall behind and a table on each side of me. This gives me a fighting chance, but I know I'm in a no-win position.

Standing and waiting, I spin my blade in my right hand. One of my tells that I'm nervous, but these assholes don't know that.

A man walks forward, and I notice he's the one from the diner, Axel, President of this club, I presume. He's intimidating as hell, over six feet, built like a brick shithouse, and if I'm truthful, I don't think I can take him down, but I'll try if I have to.

"You can put your blade away Miriam, we don't want to hurt you," he says, coming to a stop in front of me but staying far enough back I couldn't reach him if I tried.

"What the fuck do you want with me? Why am I here?" I snarl at him. If he thinks I'm going to play nice, he can take a long walk off a short pier.

"Answers, I want answers," he states calmly.

"Answers to what?" I ask, watching one of the men moving closer to me on my right, and I turn my right arm out more, still holding the blade, and glance at him so he knows I've noticed.

"Answers to what happened to have you sent to prison for something I don't think you did," he responds.

Turning to look at Axel, I cannot understand why he would want to know about that after nearly six years.

"Why, what difference does it make to you. It's done, I've served my time, and I'm moving on with my life," I state, "My name is Mia now. Miriam doesn't exist anymore. That person died the day they locked her up."

"Our club often helps women that need someone in their corner. When I heard what happened to you all that time ago, it just never rang true, but no one was talking, and I mean no one," he says, then sits at the table to my left.

"Seeing you at the diner triggered a memory, and I wasn't sure if it was you, but after looking into your prison records and the newspaper reports, we knew it was you, but we also knew something wasn't right. So here you are, and I want to know what the fuck happened."

"Well, bully for you, I don't want to go through it all again. I want to leave and move on. I'm heading as far away from here as I can get." I say, turning once again to point my blade at this one on my right.

"No, you're not, not until I get my answers." Axel states, then lunges forward and grabs the arm with the blade.

Disarmed, I have no way to get out of here, so I do the next best thing and close my mouth. I'm not saying another fucking word.

Axel asks me various questions, including do I want a drink or anything to eat, but I don't respond. I stare at a spot over his shoulder and remain quiet.

Half an hour later, Axel has obviously lost patience and tells my jailer as I think of him to take me back to the bedroom. Taking my arm, he leads me back, and when he closes the door, I hear the lock turn.

Well fuck, now what am I going to do.

CHAPTER ELEVEN

-:- CRACK -:-

Arriving at the prison, I wait while Glue checks in to see if they have a direction we can start looking. We know she was released, but where would she go from here. My understandings are either a halfway house or out on her own.

Gunner is tapping his foot, getting worked up. He better not start a thing regarding Miriam until at least we know the truth of what happened. I'd take great delight in putting this fucker on his ass.

Forty minutes later and Glue returns, smiling at us, "She caught the bus and went to the halfway house. I have the address."

Starting up my bike, I wait for everyone else to get moving, then follow along. I want to keep my eye on Gunner, which means keeping him in front of me, not behind.

We drive through the town, and it's busy, so we have to take our time, and we all pile up in front of the halfway house, parking our bikes and heading inside.

Runner walks up to the desk and gives the woman a bright smile, "Good day, we're looking for a friend who left prison a few weeks ago. Her name is Miriam Williams, the prison told us she came here, but do you know where she went from this point?"

"I'm sorry, I can't give you information regarding anyone that uses the halfway house. It's just not ethical," she states, looking down her nose at us.

"What if we gave you a donation for the house?" Tin asks her, sidling up and opening his wallet.

"Now you want to bribe me?" she starts to stand, but Gunner steps forward.

"Look, we're trying to find my daughter, she's gone missing, we believe she's trying to find Miriam, but she's only twelve, she could get into trouble." Gunner states, leaning on the desk.

I see some form of recognition when Gunner said she was twelve, so I step forward, "You've seen her, was she alright? We've got to find her. She's not streetwise, so she's not goin' to be able to protect herself."

"Maybe you should have looked after her better," she states, giving Gunner a nasty look, and if it weren't such a shit situation, I would have taken great pleasure in her comment, "But she has protection; she won't get hurt."

"What do you mean?" I ask, "Who or what is protecting her?"

"She has her very own Green Beret with her, and no one will hurt her, not even any of you." she presses a button on the side of her desk, "I suggest you leave before security arrives, or you'll find yourself in lockup."

We all head outside and sit astride our bikes. Not knowing which way we should go now, where is she and who is with her?

"Let's find something to eat, as my stomach thinks my throat's been cut." Tin states, "We need to call in and update Sharp too."

We find a drive-thru further along the road, so we pull in, use their restroom, and fill our stomachs. Runner updates Sharp on how we're doing, and Gunner is getting more and more miserable.

"All we can do now is start putting rubber to the road and see who knows a special forces man or woman that has a young girl with them. It's worth a shot as we've fuck all else." I state, starting up my bike. I head back to the main road before parking, then walking and speaking to anyone and everyone.

-:- ZARA -:-

Waking up, I feel dirty and hungry. Looking over, I see Target sitting near the window watching outside. "Good morning, Target," I say as I stand and tidy up the blankets.

"Did you sleep alright?" I ask him as he stands and moves away from the window.

"Good as ever," he says, running his hands over his hair.

"I need to go to the bathroom," and I get some wipes out of my backpack and a toothbrush, I forgot toothpaste, but at least I can give them some sort of clean.

Target opens the door and watches me get into the bathroom safely, and then I hear him walk away. I'm pleased about that as I don't want him listening to me pee.

Once we are back on the street, walking towards the diner the woman told us about, I notice Target seems quiet, and his eyes are darting everywhere.

"We need to get breakfast, Target. I've got the money, so where can we eat?" I ask him just as my stomach makes a massive rumble.

"We'll pass a breakfast food place on the way, and we can get something as we pass. They give food out to homeless people, so keep your money in your pocket," he tells me.

Nodding, I understand. I comment, "The diner people may give us something too so that we can fill our stomachs up."

I notice Target gives a half-grin when I say that, and I nudge him with my shoulder smiling at him.

"What do you think will happen when you find this friend of yours?" Target asks me, giving me an eyebrow lift.

"I don't know. I have to say I'm sorry to her." I say with some shame in my voice.

"You can tell me about it later when we get to rest awhile," he says and places a hand on my shoulder, giving it a light squeeze.

We walk for another half an hour not speaking, but it's not an uncomfortable silence. I'm looking at all the houses and streets as we walk, but I don't think I'll remember any of this later.

Target nods at a small food shop with a small line of people waiting to be served. I don't know what they are getting, but it smells pretty good.

We stand at the end of the line and wait our turn. The woman in front of me doesn't smell very nice, so I step back a little and slightly behind Target. I think he knows why I've moved as I see the side of his mouth kicked up into a bit of a smirk.

Target looks back at me, and I grin and shrug my shoulders, showing him I don't care I'm not standing close to her; she stinks.

A man stands in line behind us and leans into us, speaking quietly, "Peter, someone is looking for you. A man with a young girl is what they were looking for. Bikers have been looking at the halfway house. Keep your eyes peeled."

Target nods at the man, and we get our hot drink, which I think is coffee, and a good slice of breakfast casserole. We take our breakfast and walk over to a bench that is now in the early morning sun.

Target looks sideways at me, "Bikers Zara?"

I blow out a breath, "My dad is a biker, and all my uncles, who aren't real uncles, live there; it's the Rogue Legion MC. If they are here, then my dad is looking for me. But Target, he hasn't had any time for me in years, my mother hits me, and I've been hiding from her. I want to find Miriam. She'll look after me. She'll save me."

"Okay, tell me the story, all the story," Target asks as he finishes his breakfast and sips his coffee.

"When I was a baby, my mother Cara had me then left the hospital. I didn't see her again until I was seven. My dad looked after me on his own, well with his club brothers until I was two, then Miriam and my dad got together.

"She was my mother in all ways, she looked after me, she used to sing to me and take me everywhere. I really loved her.

"Then when I was seven Cara came back, she rushed into the house screaming and shouting, I don't know what she was saying, but she hit me and then she pulled a knife out from somewhere.

"Miriam rushed to me when Cara hit me and pushed her back, then when Cara pulled the knife screaming and trying to stab at me, Miriam was fighting with her, and she got the knife and stabbed Cara.

"Then my dad ran into the room, and Cara screamed, saying Miriam attacked her because she was jealous of her and me being her daughter. I kept trying to tell them no, she hadn't, but no one would listen, and I was carried out of the room.

"The next thing I knew, Miriam was taken and was in prison for stabbing Cara. Then Cara was living with us again, and she is horrid.

She calls me names, blames me that dad doesn't want her because it's all my fault.

"I've not spoken to any of them since then, not one word. I don't want to talk to them as they wouldn't listen."

"How long ago was all this?" Target asks.

"Five years. I'm nearly thirteen now." I state, "I need to find Miriam and tell her I'm sorry."

"Did you never try in all those years to tell the truth?" he asks, looking directly at me.

"No, I just didn't speak at all."

"You could have talked to someone at some time. You may have saved your friend from staying in prison." Target states in a low voice.

"I wish I had, but I didn't." and I have tears running down my cheeks.

"The thing is, Zara, you could have got the truth out if you tried harder. You could have stood in the middle of those men and shouted, *she didn't do it*." he states, "Someone would have listened. She may not want to have a friendship with you now, and you have to be prepared for that. Five years is a long time. She must have suffered for something she didn't do. She will be bitter about it, I would think. But we can find her, and you can at least tell her you're sorry."

I cry quietly and nod as I know I have to say sorry, and I think I already lost my friend and, worse, the person who was a mother to me.

"Come on, let's go find this diner. Worry about everything else when we need to," Target says, then places his arm around my shoulders, and we start walking, "We need to get a wash before we stink like that woman." and when I look up at him, we both burst out laughing.

CHAPTER TWELVE

-:- AXEL -:-

Damn woman, closed her mouth and now won't respond at all. But when you think about it, I can't blame her, grabbed off the street and drugged.

"Buzz, Mav, get your asses in the office," I bellow.

Standing behind my desk, I'm about ready to explode with anger. When Buzz and Mav enter, I point at the chairs for them to sit.

Walking to the office door, I close it quietly, which is far more than I'm feeling inside. When I'm standing behind my desk once more, I look at them both and then explode.

"What the fuck do you think you were doing, grabbing her off the street like that, fuckin' knocking her out with drugs. I told you to get her and bring her here, not fuckin' kidnap her. Now we've no chance of her talkin' to us." and I slam myself down into my chair.

"Pres," Buzz starts to speak.

"Shut the fuck up." I snarl at him, giving him my you're fucked look.

Mav sits forward in his chair, "We're sorry, Pres, but it was the quickest and cleanest way to get her at the time. She was just about to climb onto another bus, and we couldn't take the chance. No one was around, so we just grabbed her."

"It's fucked up, is what it is," I state, leaning back in my chair and pulling at the back of my hair in frustration.

"Sorry, Axel, we did what we thought would be quickest and cleanest at the time," Buzz says, leaning forward with his elbows on his knees.

"Well, we can't change it now, but I'm not sure she'll trust us now. I'll go talk to her and see what I can find out if anything." standing and walking to the door.

Walking through the main room, you can tell the difference since we had Church, the place is much cleaner, and the club girls are staying out of the way, not laying around on the furniture all day long.

Heading upstairs, I see Brag sitting on the chair opposite the room we have Miriam in. He stands when he sees me coming towards him.

"Anything to report?" I ask.

"No, it's been all quiet," he responds.

"Okay, go grab yourself a drink and bring it back here with you. We may need something brought for Miriam, so keep someone in the kitchen alert, and you can text them if I get any progress in here." I move to the door and turn the key, take a deep breath and enter.

Miriam is sitting on the window sill, looking out into the yard below. She makes no sign of hearing me enter.

The room has a queen-size bed, dresser, chair, and small walk-in closet, plus a bath—all in all, a nice room.

"Is everything okay for you in here?" I ask, but again no response.

Sitting on the edge of the bed facing her, I know I've got to get her talking, but she's gonna be a stubborn one, I'm sure.

"Miriam, I'm sorry that you were brought here in the way you were. It wasn't my intention at all. The men just got carried away with it all.

"As a club, when we hear of women being mistreated, we do whatever we can to get them out of that situation. It's not an official job of the club. We just do what we can, when we can.

"When this thing happened to you, I saw it in the newspapers and heard things whispered, but nothing ever came to me as concrete evidence.

"Five years you spent inside, and I believe you're innocent, and if that's true, I want to help you clear your name, find the one who should have had the sentence."

All the time I'm speaking, she says nothing, doesn't even turn to speak to me, look at me or show any kind of response at all.

"Are you hungry or thirsty? I'll send up whatever you fancy if we have it." I offer, but again no response.

"Okay, I'll talk to you again later," I turn to the door, and as I'm going to open it, I turn back to her, "You won't be leaving here until you talk to me, so the quicker you do, the quicker you can get out of here." and with that, I walk out and lock the door once more.

"How did it go?" Brag asks from his chair opposite.

"Nothin', I'll try again later. Just keep your ears peeled." and I walk away, back to the office. Now I'm wondering if I should call Sharp and let him know I have her or wait to see how this plays out.

-:- ZARA -:-

I think my legs are going to fall off, we've walked and walked, and I've no idea how far. I just know I'm going to fall over if we walk much further.

"Target? We nearly there?" I ask hopefully.

"About ten minutes, I think. Are you alright, or do you need to rest a minute?" he asks, looking down at me with a slight smirk.

"I'm okay. We can keep walking." I say because I don't want him thinking I'm a baby and can't walk this far.

Nodding, Target carries on walking but has a little kick up on the side of his mouth. Shit, I'll show him I can make it, and I dig in and keep putting one foot in front of the other.

The diner is right on the edge of town, amongst a few other shops, not many but a small food store, laundromat, and looks like a gun shop.

Entering the diner, we walk over to the counter, and a nice-looking lady smiles at us.

"Can we have two drinks, please?" I ask, then plop down in the nearest booth.

Target chuckles and tells her we want a soda and a coffee, then sits in the opposite seat to mine. "You, okay?" he asks, grinning.

"I'm okay. My legs are just tired." I admit at last, "I'm hungry too. Shall we have something to eat while we're here?"

"Yeah, okay, we can eat. Do you have enough money left? I can get some cash if we need it. My pay still goes into my account, although I don't use it." Target tells me.

"I've got quite a bit left. It's my savings from birthdays and Christmas, so I have a good bit," I tell him smiling.

The lady brings our drinks, and I ask, "Do you have a deep-dish pizza with lots of cheese on top and fries?"

"We sure do. We have one large enough for you to share and a good heap of fries on the side," she states, smiling at me.

Looking over at Target, "Do you fancy sharing that?" I ask, and he nods with a smile.

That's when we just sit back and rest a little while as we wait for our lunch. I know I've got to speak to the lady, but I'm going to eat first in case she chucks us out.

The pizza was amazing. It had pepperoni, mushrooms, sweet peppers, and three different kinds of cheese, all stringy when you bite into it.

Once we've finished our meal, I walk over to the register and pay the lady, Target steps up behind me, and I take a deep breath and quickly say, "Do you know if Miriam worked here for you? She is my friend, and I'm trying to find her? We don't want to cause trouble or hurt her. I just want to find her to say I'm sorry."

The lady looks at us both closely, "Please, sit down again for a minute." and she calls to the man in the kitchen, "Graham, come out here a minute."

With no one else in the diner, the lady walks over to the door and locks it turning the sign to say the diner is closed.

She and the man sit down with us, and the man turns to Target, "My name is Graham, this is my wife, Suzie. We do know Miriam, but she is called Mia now. She is no longer here. Two biker clubs have been here in the last few months, and one asked for Miriam; that is when she left. We don't know where she is. We just know she caught the first bus of the day."

Suzie looks at us both hard, "If you're here to have her hurt, I'll find a way to hurt you both. I don't care you're a child, you could have saved her, and I won't let you hurt her again."

Target leans forward, "We have no intention of hurting her. Zara just wants to say she's sorry for her part in all that happened, which was allowing herself to be ignored when she tried to speak up. Do you know the name of the two biker clubs that were in here?"

Graham nods, "Yes, one was Raging Barons MC, and the other was Rogue Legion MC."

"Rogues are my dad's club. If dad finds her first, he'll hurt her." I say and start to cry.

"They didn't ask for her. The other one did. If the Rogue's come back, I won't tell them anything if they are trying to find her to hurt her." Graham states and Suzie is nodding in agreement.

We thank them and leave the diner, walking back towards the town. Looking up at Target, I can see he is deep in thought, so I keep quiet.

"Come on, little sister, let's go talk to some people and find out where we can find these Raging Barons." Target states, and he wraps his arm around my shoulders, and we increase our pace a little more.

CHAPTER THIRTEEN

-:- MIA -:-

Sitting on the window sill, my stomach is starting to growl, but I just want out of this damn place. The men in the yard keep looking up at me, but I don't give them any sign that I see them.

How the hell am I going to get out of here? I don't understand why these people care about what happened to me. It makes no sense at all.

The window is bolted shut, and apart from trying to break the glass and fall to the ground, there's no way out of here.

Entering the bathroom, I turn on the shower to warm up and take out a clean set of clothes. Jeans, a t-shirt and a sweater will do.

I don't see anything to dry my hair, and with the length, it's going to take a long time to dry on its own. I rub with a towel to get as much water out as I can, then brush it over and over to try and get air to it. Maybe it's time to have it cut shorter. I don't know.

Sitting on the window sill brushing my hair to try and help it dry faster, my arms are starting to ache. I carry on for a few more minutes, then braid it to keep it out of the way.

My stomach gives another large growl, and I'm starting to feel a little sickly with hunger, but fuck it, I'm not getting anything from this lot. They drugged me once; they're not drugging me again.

Walking into the bathroom, I run the cold water at the hand basin and scoop my hands together, holding as much water as I can, then drink until I feel my stomach is sloshing around, but it's stopped that hungry feeling for the time being.

Making sure my dirty clothes are back in my backpack, I leave it near the door. I want it handy to grab when I leave this place.

Sitting back on the window sill, I let a sigh slip out but rest my head against the glass and close my eyes for a little while.

Memories of being inside play through my mind. One woman was determined to make my life miserable and as hard as possible. She stopped after I cornered her in the shower, she didn't dare tell anyone what had happened either, in case I went back for more, but her broken arm told a story.

I'm not the same person anymore. I loved helping people, worked hard to get the job at the bank, now I'll never be able to do that again. All this happened because I loved Gunner and Zara, but never again, the bitterness is ripe now, and I'm not sure I'll ever get rid of it.

I'm sad because it's not who I am. I fought through foster care and came out still optimistic of a promising future, worked hard to build that for myself, then I was stupid enough to allow a man and his daughter into my heart.

Rubbing my back with my hands, I shake the memories and thoughts. I don't want to linger on all that happened. I want to leave it behind me and move on. I have to get out of here first.

Hearing voices outside the door, I keep my face toward the window, blowing out a calming breath, ready for whoever may enter the room.

I hear the lock turn, and someone enters. The smell of food enters with them, but I don't look.

"Hi, my name is Candy, and I brought you a meal and some coffee." she squeaks out. That is the only way you can describe it, squeaky and high-pitched.

Looking at her reflection in the window, I have to stop myself from smirking. She has on a crop top that hardly covers her tits and a pair of shorts that are no wider than a belt, fucking club whore is my guess.

Dyed blonde, cut in a bob, fake as shit tits, and so thin she needs a god-damn healthy meal. She can't be more than five-one if she's an inch.

"Are you not going to speak to me?" she says, stepping nearer to me.

I remain silent and don't turn to her to acknowledge her in any way, she's still stepping closer, and I'm watching carefully in the window as to what she has planned.

The door opens again, and Candy whirls around to see who has entered when a deep voice firmly says, "Candy, get outta here, you've delivered the food, now move."

I presume it's the man who's on guard, but I don't speak or turn towards them. I keep my vigilance on their reflections until they've left the room and the door is locked again.

I'm not sure if I should eat the food or not. Do I risk being drugged again? Fucking hell, I'm in a bad position as I don't know how long they intend to keep me here, and I can't afford to get weak in case I have to fight.

Walking over and taking the dome cover off the plate, the meal of chicken and side vegetables looks reasonably safe, well I hope it is.

I decide to take the risk and eat quickly, then drink the can of soda rather than the hot drink, which looks like weak coffee.

Sitting on the window sill once more, I rest my head on the glass and watch the people below, but it's not long before tiredness overtakes me, and I fall asleep.

-:- CRACK -:-

Walking through the town, we ask as many people as we can if they have seen a thirteen-year-old girl who may be asking where to find a friend. A couple of times, I think someone knows something, but they won't tell.

Meeting up at the drive-thru, we get enough food to feed ourselves twice, then sit on a bench to eat and drink soda. As I'm eating, I'm scanning around to see if anything may give me a clue as to which way Zara would have walked, but nothing jumps out at me.

"What do you all think? Are we on the right track?" I ask, and I have to admit I don't know what will be the best way to find her now.

"We can keep asking, maybe look for some street kids; they know more than you think. We could throw 'em a few bucks that may loosen lips." Runner suggests.

"Okay, let's get moving again before it gets too late," I state and throw my garbage in the barrel next to the bench.

We walk quite a way, asking everyone we meet, then I notice a young kid leaning against fencing before a park entrance. I walk over and give him a nod, "Have you seen a man with a kid, she's about thirteen, my niece and his daughter," pointing to Gunner, who is walking towards us, "I can throw you a few bucks if you can get us on the right road, we've been looking in town all day and need to find her before something happens to her.

"We were told she has a man with her who was a Green Beret, but we don't know him, and neither did she."

"If you can help at all, we would appreciate it."

The kid stands and holds his hand out, and I get forty dollars out of my wallet. I hold it out but don't let him take it.

"Peter was with her. He'll keep her safe. They were going towards the diner, from what I heard. They were asking about a woman who may have worked for them." he wriggles his fingers for me to give him the money, "That's all I know. The diner is that way, the last diner before you leave town. But they'll be closed now."

I hand over the money, and he runs off. Turning to Gunner and the others, they are looking as tired as I am.

"Let's head back to our bikes, then find a motel, get some rest. First thing in the morning, we'll go to this diner and find out what they know," I state and start walking back through the town.

It's probably going to take us forty minutes to walk back to our damn bikes. Gunner is moaning and cursing as we go, but no one is taking any notice. We're all too tired to argue with him.

"Do you think he was telling the truth, Crack?" Tin asks.

"Well, he had no reason to lie, and it sounded plausible, but who is this, Peter? I don't know. I just hope he's keeping her safe," I respond and slow my walk as my legs are damn tired. We must have covered over ten miles today.

"I'll fuckin' kill him if he hurts her," Gunner growls, "I'm gonna kill her for disappearing and causing all this shit."

"You'll not touch her. You need to learn to listen to her, and she would never run to find Miriam if Miriam had ever hurt her; think on that, Gunner. She running to Miriam and away from Cara and you, what does that tell you?" and after dropping that on him, I pick up my speed and leave him stewing it over behind me.

CHAPTER FOURTEEN

-:- AXEL -:-

Time to get some answers, and I hope Miriam is more receptive when I go back upstairs. Sending Candy with a meal may soften her up a little, but I'm guessing at this point in time.

As I walk out of my office, Silver walks towards me, "Pres, my street guy told me he'd seen a man with a girl that sounds like it could be the one missing from Rogue Legion MC. Do you want me to go check it out?"

"Yes, see if we can't get some fuckin' answers. If we can find the girl, then maybe this whole thing will get unraveled and Silver, if we find that the woman upstairs was railroaded, we're gonna talk to our Judge, get him to earn his fuckin' pay for once." I respond, starting to walk away once more, only to hear the phone ringing in my office.

Silver is my guy in contact with all our street guys. Anything we need to know on the street, he can find out. He's six feet of solid muscle; he loves the gym and working out in general.

Damn and blast it, I think to myself, always fuckin' something stopping me getting things done. Dashing back to my desk, I grab the telephone and snap out, "What?"

"Is this a bad time, Axel? It's Sharp just checking in to see if you've found anythin'?"

"We just had news that we could have a sighting of the young girl you're looking for. One of mine has gone out to see what they can find. If it's her, I'll let you know." and I slam the phone down before he can ask anything else.

The last thing I want is his club coming here demanding they take Miriam. No fucking way on my watch is that happening. They let her down once; they're fucking not doing it again.

Trying again to go upstairs to get answers, I am once more waylaid by Specs, "Pres, can I talk to you a minute?"

"Yeah, what's up, man?" I say as I follow him into his office.

Specs closes the door behind me and points for me to sit. Stepping behind his desk, he lifts a piece of paper which I can see has his scrawling, spidery writing on.

"Okay, Pres, Sting was talking to his sister who works in the homeless food shop. He asked if she'd seen anyone, and she said she saw a homeless man she knew that had a young girl with him. They ate breakfast and then left." Passing me the piece of paper, "His name is Peter, and she knows he's called Peter Faulke, but he is also called 'Target' because he was a Green Beret, and they say he never missed his target.

"Is this following the information we know so far, Pres? I think it is, anyway, looking up Peter Faulke. He indeed was a Green Beret. He was injured during his last tour when his team was killed, all but one other.

"He was awarded the Purple Heart and a Silver Star. I don't think for a minute this guy will hurt the girl. In fact, God help anyone that tries while she's with him.

"He's twenty-four, no family, seems he's been protecting some of the homeless around here."

"Good work Specs, this at least puts our mind at rest a little. We now need to find him because finding him will find her." I stand and turn to the door, looking back over my shoulder, "Any more information about Miriam, her time in prison, or the run-up to her incarceration?"

"No, sorry Pres, as of yet no more than we knew." Specs states then sits back behind his computer screen.

Before anyone can waylay me again, I head straight for the stairs and run up two steps at a time. Sitting outside Miriam's door on guard is Hammer, legs stretched well across the hallway, arms folded and looking well and truly bummed, I can't help it, but the look on his face has me smirking.

"Go grab a drink, Hammer. I'll wait here until you get back. I'm gonna see if I can get our guest talking." I state, turning the key, and opening the door.

Walking in, I note that her head is laying on the glass window, and her eyes are closed. Looking down, I can see she ate the meal. I'm pleased as she's been here a long time now to have had nothing.

Picking up the tray, I open the door and place it on the floor so someone can pick it up and take it down. Then turn and re-enter the bedroom.

I sit on the end of the bed facing the window and notice that Miriam now has her eyes open, looking directly at me.

"Did you enjoy the meal? If you need anything, you can knock on the door and ask Hammer who's outside." I state, then fold my arms, stretch out my legs and let her see I'm not going anywhere anytime soon.

As she has been since we put her in this room, still saying nothing. She turns and looks back out of the window.

"Miriam, you'll be in here until you answer my questions. I don't want to hurt you in any way. I just want to know the truth. This case bugged me right back when it happened, and it's still bugging me.

"Your old MC is looking for you. Is it Gunner that you were involved with at the time? Well, he's lookin' and not in any good way.

"His daughter Zara has gone missing. They think she ran off to try and find you as she just heard you were released from prison." I notice she swallows, and her shoulders drop slightly on the last part, so she has feelings for this girl even after all this.

"Sharp has been in touch with me. He wants to know if we find you. So far, I've told him nothin', and I'll keep doing that until I'm happy that they won't be tryin' to hurt you at all.

"Zara is with a man who's living on the streets, but he's a good guy from what we've found out, but we have to find her before anything bad happens. If something happens to her, you know you'll get blamed for that too, even though you've had nothin' to do with it."

Miriam turns on the window sill and looks directly at me, she places her hands in her lap, and I can see her knuckles are white where she's fisting her hands so tightly.

"My name is now Mia. I don't and won't answer to Miriam," she says quietly, none of the aggression she had when she was first brought here.

"I didn't hurt Zara. Ever. She was like a daughter to me. Now, I'm moving away, the furthest from here I can get, and MCs are not something I want to be involved with ever again." she keeps her head down, looking at her hands.

"Why did they think you hurt her?" I ask.

"I don't know. I don't want to talk about this anymore." Mia turns to the window and places her forehead on the glass.

"Sharp will want to talk to you. I can't put him off forever. I can give you some time, but you'll have to face him soon." I state, but she doesn't show any sign of hearing me.

I stand and leave the room, locking it behind me, then turning to Hammer, "If she needs anythin' like a drink or whatever, let her have it, just get one of the club girls to sort it, you stay here."

Hammer nods, then settles back in his seat, "Do you think she hurt that girl Pres?"

"Not for a single minute," I respond, then head back down to my office.

-:- ZARA -:-

Target speaks to a few of his friends; they all look like they live on the street. They're friendly and talk to me even though I'm a kid.

While Target is still talking, I see a bench and walk over, sitting down and leaning back, just resting a minute. I don't think my legs have ever walked so much.

I think about my dad, and maybe he'll miss me, but then he might not even notice I've gone, and I know Cara won't care. All she wanted was a way to get back to dad and into the clubhouse.

I know she talks to someone called Snap. She calls him when dad's not around and whispers when she's talking to him. She looks through dad's kutte pockets when he's asleep or in the bathroom, I've seen her, but she doesn't want dad to see her.

Target sits next to me, pulls me into his side, and I put my head on his chest, wrapping my arms around his middle. We take a minute to rest in the sunshine.

"We have a long walk back into town, Zara. Tomorrow we need to go to the next town over, that's where we'll find the MC that may know where she is, but we can find out why they want to talk to her." Target says.

"Can we get a motel tonight? I have enough money. We can have a shower, change our clothes or buy some new ones. Then we can eat and sleep." I look up at Target with my most hopeful look.

"Are you too tired to walk back?" he asks me with a half-grin.

"Yes, my legs are tired out," I whine a bit, I'm not a baby usually, but I think I could cry.

"Okay, let's call at the bank first, let me get some cash, then we'll go to the motel. If we go to the one on the way back, they have a store, snack shop, and suites. We could have a good meal and rest," Target says, then pulls me up off the bench, and we start walking again.

As we get to within a few minutes of the motel, a man walks over and speaks to Target, "Hey man, someone's been asking about you. Two MCs, they seem to know your name, so someone's talked."

I look up at Target to see if he looks worried, but he hasn't changed his expression at all.

"It's okay, Brock, if they find me, they do, but I'm ready. This is Zara, she's a friend, and I'm watching out for her. Let it be known people need to keep it quiet, or I won't be happy." Target tells this man called Brock.

Brock walks away after giving Target a nod, and we start walking again, heading for the bank, which is just ahead thankfully as I need to stop soon, my legs feel like they will drop off.

Target leads me into the bank, and I take a seat while he walks to the counter. I look around and see people giving Target odd looks and trying not to walk past him, no idea why as he's nice, and though he does look a bit dirty, he's been kind to me.

My head is dropping a bit as I'm tired, and I can feel my eyelids starting to close. I jerk my head up and make my eyes open again. I hope Target hurries up.

Someone is shaking my shoulder gently, and I hear, "Come on, little girl, let's go to the motel, get a room and some rest."

I stand up but am a bit wobbly on my legs. Target picks up my backpack and throws it over his shoulder, then wraps his arm around my shoulders and leads me out of the bank. We head straight for the motel and a long rest, I hope.

Target gets us a suite, and we go straight to it. I take my backpack into the bathroom and have a shower, then throw myself onto the twin bed and fall asleep.

The smell of something good wakes me, and I sit up, rubbing my eyes. Looking up, Target is watching TV and has a pile of food on the coffee table in front of him.

He must have wrapped me up when I fell asleep as I'm tucked into bed tightly and have to fight to get my arms out of the covers.

Once out of bed, I walk over to Target and sit on the floor behind the coffee table. I pick up a piece of pizza and eat it fast.

"You okay, Zara? Feel any better for that sleep?" Target asks, and when I look up, I have to blink as he's had a shower and has new, clean clothes on, even had a shave, he looks so different.

"Wow, Target, you look so different." I burst out, "I hardly knew who you were." and then I grinned at him.

"Sassy little girl." Target replies but is smirking at me.

"I feel better for that sleep. I was tired. I've never walked so far." I tell him, smiling.

"You slept a long time. I've been shopping, got some new clothes, had a shower, and got food, all while you've been snoring," he says, pointing his piece of pizza at me.

"I don't snore." I gasp out.

"You sure do, loud ones. They were knocking on the wall next door telling you to shut up," he says, and I'm not sure if he's joking until I see the small crinkles at the side of his eyes which tells me he's laughing at me.

I can't help it. I giggle as he is funny when he's teasing me.

"Tomorrow we're going to visit the next town, watch what's going on at the MC. See what is happening before we go speak to them." Target looks serious now, so I nod, "We'll watch and listen. Only when we know it's okay will we speak to them.

"Let's get settled, get some sleep, and be rested for tomorrow. Can you sleep some more?"

"Yes, I'll rest if I don't sleep. I won't wake you up." I say and quickly visit the bathroom, wash and clean my teeth, then jump back into bed. "Night Target."

"Night, little girl." Target replies, then tucks me in tight once more.

CHAPTER FIFTEEN

-:- CRACK -:-

After waking from a half-decent night's sleep, we all head out to our bikes and get ready to find the diner where Miriam worked after leaving prison.

Sitting astride my bike, I turn to Gunner and give him the evil eye, "You keep your mouth shut. They won't tell us fuck all if you start mouthing off. If Miriam worked for them, they probably like her, and you sayin' anythin' nasty will just have them clam up."

Gunner gives me the stink eye, but Tin speaks up, "Yeah, I agree with you, Crack, Miriam was easy to like, she worked hard, she helped everyone if she's still the same, they'll like her, and if we're disrespectful, they won't tell us a thing."

Glue and Runner are nodding agreement, so I look over at Gunner, who doesn't look happy but nods his agreement too.

Riding through town, I keep my eyes peeled and see a couple of Raging Baron's MC men on the streets. Now that's interesting, what are they looking for?

I know Sharp has been speaking to Axel, the Raging Baron's MC President, mainly because they do a bit of white knight shit, saving women from abusive husbands, that type of thing. I applaud them for it but not sure why they want to be involved in this situation.

A bike riding up alongside shows a Raging Baron giving us the eye, letting us know they've seen us in their area. Thankfully Sharp got permission for us to be here and wear our kuttes, or we'd have a brawl right now.

The biker sticks with us for a few streets then bursts forward and leaves us in his wake. Glue drops back and looks over to me, giving me the signal to turn off in a minute, and as he checks where the diner is, I'm happy to follow wherever he leads.

Pulling up in front of the diner, I realize it's the diner where I saw the waitress that looked familiar, shit, that could have been her, and I let her slip through my fingers.

On entering, the woman smiles and gets ready to pour coffee from the pot into cups. I make sure to smile at her and nod, then lead the others to a table near the window rather than one of the booths that only holds four people.

The woman brings our cups and coffee, filling them up and handing us menus before walking back to the counter.

I keep my eye on her, but she shows no sign of nervousness, which may mean I was wrong about Miriam being here. She places dirty dishes on the hatch, which a man in the kitchen picks up, and then she washes down a couple of tables before walking back to us with a pad in her hand.

"What can I get you? Have you decided?" the woman asks, and that's when I notice her hand is shaking slightly as she holds her pen over the pad in her other hand.

"I'll have the full breakfast with a side of white toast," I state, keeping my eye on her.

The others place their orders, and she keeps the smile and is polite. Maybe it's just our kuttes that's making her nervous and not what I'm thinking.

Tin leans over to me, "Did she look nervous? I noticed her hands were a little shaky."

"Yeah, I noticed that, but it could be just our kuttes. you know, some people are nervous about us. Let's just eat and let her relax. I'll speak to her before we leave. When I pay the bill may be the best time." I respond quietly, keeping my voice as low as I can.

The woman keeps busy, but nothing that I would think she wasn't supposed to be doing anyway. Bringing our meals over, she smiles and speaks as you would expect. Nothing about her says she is hiding anything.

We all relax and enjoy breakfast. The man in the kitchen can cook. It has none of that greasy taste to it at all. Holding my cup up, the woman brings the pot and tops me off with a smile.

Another half an hour and the place is empty apart from us. I lean over and tell them to stand by the bikes, and I'll pay and speak to the woman and the man in the back if necessary.

They all thank the woman and walk out, standing around the bikes and looking relaxed.

"That was a great breakfast," looking at her name tag, "Thanks, Suzie, we enjoyed it, and I'm sure we'll be back again." I pay her and make sure I place a large tip on the counter.

"Can I ask if you've seen a young woman called Miriam? We've been led to believe she worked here after leaving prison. We wish her no harm. It's just that a young girl has gone missing while looking for her, and we're worried about where she is and if she's safe." I let her see how worried I am and lean onto the counter, "I also want to try and prove Miriam's innocence. I truly believe she didn't do what she was incarcerated for.

"The woman who she stabbed, I think, set her up, or at the least lied about what happened. I knew Miriam and never believed she would hurt Zara, but we were all told to leave it alone at the time.

"Now, I'm not willing to keep quiet. If I can get justice for her and clear her name, I'd like to do that at least, I'm sure she's suffered, and that cuts me."

"We've had others here asking the same questions; we don't know who to believe, but we can tell you that although we didn't know much about Mia, she would never hurt a child, and if you people were supposed to know her you should have known that and stood up for her, not watch her go to prison for something she didn't do," Suzie states with some venom in her voice.

"You called her Mia. Has she changed her name?" I ask, taking the woman by surprise as I don't think up to now, she realized she'd dropped that piece of information.

"I would like you to leave now. I have nothing more to tell you." she states and walks to the door, opening it and looking pointedly at me, "Come back some time for another meal." she says and closes it behind me once I've walked out.

Reaching my bike, I turn to my brothers, "She changed her name to Mia, and I think we need to speak to Raging Baron's MC now. We've run out of information." I state grimly.

-:- MIA -:-

I've been two days locked in this room, and I'm about ready to go stir crazy, but I'm not telling Axel any more than I have already. If he thinks I'm going to talk to him and then more people, he can think again. I'm ready to break this window and escape, and I'm crazy enough to do it.

Walking into the bathroom, I turn the faucet on over the sink and start to fill it while opening my backpack and taking out the underwear I need to get washed as I'm on my last clean pair now.

There is no bar soap, so I grab the shower gel and squirt enough into the water to wash these few items out. Once clean, I rinse well, then wring them out and hang them on the side of the tub to dry out. Thankfully the bathroom is pretty warm, so it should help them dry before morning.

Shaking out my clothes, I can see they are reasonably clean, and I'll need to find a laundromat when I leave here as I'm going to be wearing my last clean pair of jeans and a t-shirt when I've had a shower.

After showering and dressing, I pick up and fold the towels and leave the bathroom as clean as possible.

Walking into the bedroom, a woman in a pair of shorts that are up the crack of her ass and a crop top which has half her tits showing at the bottom and just enough at the top that her nipples aren't showing is standing looking at the few items I had left lying on the bed.

"What are you doing in here?" I ask her snappily. Nosy bitch is checking out my gear.

"I brought you food and a drink." she turns, looking me up and down, which has me smirking as she looks at me like that when she's standing there wearing hardly anything at all, "Who the fuck are you?" she asks.

"No one, now get the fuck out." I snarl at her, walking over to the door and throwing it open, which has the man in the chair opposite jumping up in case I do a runner.

"What's goin' on?" he asks, looking from one of us to the other.

"Nothing, she was just leaving." and I push the woman out and slam the door.

Hearing the key turn, I know the door is locked again, so I walk over to the bed and place everything back into my backpack. I think to myself. I'm getting out of here tomorrow, even if I have to climb out of a broken window.

Taking the dome cover off the food, I see a nasty breakfast, oatmeal with lumps in it. No way am I eating that shit.

Picking up the coffee, I once more sit on the window sill and watch men coming and going. Then I notice the skank that was in here a while ago, she's standing behind the dumpster and using a cell phone, and that's when I see her looking up at me.

Yep, I've got that feeling, she's reporting back to someone, so one of the Rogue Legion MC or someone else is the question. Either way, I'm getting out of here soon.

The lock turns once more, and the door opens to reveal none other than Axel. I turn back to the window when I know who it is, not going to play any more games with him or anyone else.

Axel sits on the end of the bed once more and watches me for a while, "If you're innocent, why would Cara, the mother set you up? Do you have any idea at all?"

I turn to look at him. He can't ask me anything I haven't asked myself a hundred times while being in prison. I don't want to play his games, so I just shrug my shoulder.

Axel asks me one question after another, and I just keep shrugging my shoulder. At the end of the day, I have no answers to the questions.

"We need to get all the players together and find out what happened and why. I think Zara has answers if we ask her the right questions." Axel states, but I just keep my face without emotion and look out the window.

"I'm not giving up on this, Mia. It's five years too late getting the truth told. You need it told so you can have closure," he says, then stands and walks back to the door.

"There is no closure on it, Axel. I've paid dearly, and I won't ever forgive them. People that said they were my family, people that were supposed to have my back. I'll go it alone from now on. At least then I can blame myself and not other people when things go wrong." I state quietly but mean every single word.

"You need to move on once your name is cleared. MCs are about family, watching out for each other, supporting each other. If that didn't happen for you, then they don't deserve you ever to forgive them, but you can't hate everyone for what a few did. That's not healthy." Axel says, then quietly closes the door.

CHAPTER SIXTEEN

-:- ZARA -:-

Waking up in a bed is pretty good. I look over the top cover and see Target sitting at the window, he has a drink, and a bag with something in that smells pretty good.

"Morning, Target," I say as I sit up and rub my eyes. Oh, my legs are aching when I move them to hang over the edge of the bed.

"Morning, Zara," turning to look at me, "Get a quick wash up and come eat your breakfast. I got you a breakfast casserole, pretty good too."

Rushing into the bathroom, I do what I need to, wash up and clean my teeth. Re-entering the bedroom, I walk over and pick up the foil-wrapped meal, then sit on the end of the bed to eat.

"How do you feel this morning? Do your legs ache?" Target asks with a slight grin.

"Yes, but I'll be okay," I tell him with a smile. I'm not going to complain; I'm not a little girl anymore.

"We can get a cab, and then we'll have to be on our feet to find somewhere to watch. Once we know it's safe, we can go and speak to them, but not before," Target says, turning once more to look at me, "You'll do exactly what I say, Zara. I can't keep you safe if you don't agree to that."

"I will, I promise."

"Okay, then, I won't let anyone or anything hurt you. But I need you to do as I say, keep our heads down, don't be seen until we're ready." Target insists.

He has that sound to his voice that my dad has when he's being serious and taking no shit, so I know I have to be good.

We finish eating and make sure we've picked up all our things before we head outside.

"Let's take the key back, and then we can catch a cab." Target states, and I follow him to the reception.

I wait outside while he goes in, looking around as he told me to watch for anything out of the ordinary. I'm not sure I'm any good at this, but I'll try to do as he says.

It's only a few minutes before Target comes back out, and he points to the main gateway, "We can wait there for the cab; the woman on reception called one for us."

"Okay. Do you need me to give you money for the room?" I ask as I have some left from my savings.

"No, little girl, I got it," he says, smiling at me, then places his arm around my shoulders as we walk.

As we're standing waiting, I'm trying to remember the last time my dad wrapped his arm around my shoulders, hugged me, or even spoke to me, and I'm not sure.

Cara is always drinking or sticking that tube up her nose, she must be sick, but I daren't ask as she hit me last time I did.

Dad doesn't come to the house anymore. He stays in the clubhouse. That's why I have my hiding place. It's better than being at home with Cara.

The cab arrives, and we both climb in, Target tells the man where we want to go, and I make sure my backpack is on the floor behind my legs before I place my belt on.

Target is sitting in the front with the driver, and they are talking about the scenery, I think, but I'm not listening. Adult stuff is pretty dull when I've bothered to listen.

The carryall that Target has is pretty big, so he put that in the trunk. I'm not sure what he has in it. I didn't bother to ask.

We are dropped off near a small diner, and Target tells me we're going to pick up some stuff to eat and drink while we do our surveillance. Well, I think that's what he called it, and I think he means we keep watch.

Target picks up protein bars, chips, a couple of chocolate bars, soda, and water. It has me wondering how long we're going to be watching these people.

We get most of the things into my backpack, and Target helps me get it on. I'm not complaining even though it is heavy.

Across from the Raging Barons MC clubhouse, Target has us sneaking to a place where we won't be seen. He cuts up some bushes and makes us a little den. He places a blanket on the ground, and we sit, waiting and watching.

Target takes out a pair of binoculars. He even lets me look when I ask. It's pretty neat as they look so near when you look through these things.

"Have you ever seen Lord of The Rings, Target?" I ask to which he shakes his head; he hasn't, "Well, I feel like Frodo Baggins on a quest." I tell him with a smirk.

"Tell me about it," Target asks.

I spend the next hour telling Target all about the movies, what happens, and how much I liked them. Even the horrid wizard man, how he scared me and I didn't go to sleep one night after seeing a big eye every time I closed my eyes.

After a while, we have a bag of chips and a drink of water. Then I settle back, waiting while Target is watching through his binoculars again. I don't think it takes long before I fall asleep.

Now and again, I wake up to the sound of motorbikes, but at Target's headshake, I settle back down again and carry-on napping.

-:- AXEL -:-

I know we're on limited time before Sharp or someone else will catch on to the fact we have Mia here at the compound. If I could get answers from her, it would help me know if I should let her go or keep her here until things are sorted out.

Although we have sightings reported about a man and young girl, we haven't been able to catch up with them. They keep one step ahead of us.

Sharp has left three messages for me and now wants me to call him back. He has four of his guys hanging around on our turf, and I don't want them here for months on end. I'm going to have to speak to him or have a sit-down.

Walking into my office, I'm surprised to see Buzz sitting waiting for me. As our enforcer, he is usually out and about, checking out any sign of a problem the club may have.

"Everything okay, Buzz?" I ask as I walk around my desk and take a seat.

"What we doing with that woman? Got her locked up like a prisoner Pres. Don't feel right." Buzz states in his deep, gravelly voice.

"I'm tryin' to find out the truth and keep her safe at the same time. If I let her out the room, she'll run, and we'll never clear her name." I say, and I know he's not happy with Mia being locked in a room, but I'm unsure what else to do.

"Let me try talking to her, see if a new face will help," he suggests.

"Your face is one that kidnapped her, so why would she trust you?" I ask him, not sure he even thought about that fact.

"Well, if not me, we could ask Ruger. He has a way with the women. Maybe he could sweet talk her into talkin'," Buzz stands, and that tells me he's said what he wanted to get off his chest.

"Okay, I'll speak to Ruger, see if he'll talk to her." I agree, then close the door after Buzz leaves. Picking up my cell, I message Ruger to come to my office and Fizz, one of our prospects, to bring me a shot and a beer.

A few minutes later, a knock on the door opens slightly to Fizz, saying he has my drinks. On my come in, he enters, places them on the desk, and quickly leaves.

As he is leaving, Ruger pops his head inside. "You want me, Pres?"

"Yeah, take a seat, Ruger," when he is settled, I lean forward on my desk, forearms leaning to take my weight, "I need you to do me a solid. Talk to Mia, see if you can warm her up and get her willing to tell us what happened before and once she was in prison.

"We need to know everything we can before Sharp and some of the boys turn up. He won't stay away long, and you can bet he'll find out Mia is here soon."

Ruger gives me a serious look, "I can do that Pres, don't know if she'll open up, but I can try. I'll take her next meal around eighteen hundred hours and see what I can get from her. I'll let you know when I've been."

Giving Ruger a nod of agreement, he leaves the office, and I can only hope she'll open up to him so we have something to throw at Sharp when he eventually arrives.

Throwing the shot back, I take a good drink of the beer, then pick up my cell and call Sharp.

"Yoh, what you got, Axel?" Sharp barks.

"We've not found the girl yet. We know she's with a male, an ex-Green Beret, so she's safe as far as we can tell. If she's looking for Miriam, then she may have more information than we have," I keep all information as basic as I can, "Have you any more news?"

Sharp takes a deep breath, "Crack's spoken to people at a diner. They employed her when she left prison, but she's moved on, and they didn't know where."

"So, we're still on the collect information route. Find your girl and Miriam." I state, giving nothing in my voice at all.

Closing out the call, I shove my cell into my back pocket and walk out to the main room. I need to speak to the two that took meals up to Mia.

I know Candy took one of the meals, so I walk over to her where she is leaning over the bar talking to the prospect, fucking hell, she has no panties on and showing her pussy to everyone who walks past.

"Candy!" I snap, "Go put some panties on, then come to the office," I don't want a response. I walk back to the office, shaking my head.

What the fuck is the matter with these women, who wants to sit on a seat after their bare pussy has been sitting on it? It makes me want to gag. I'm pleased I haven't used a club whore for a couple of years.

Waiting in my office, it only takes ten minutes before Candy walks in. Oh, Christ, she tries to look sultry or some shit, but she looks what she is, a skank.

"What was said when you took the meal to the woman upstairs?" I ask fairly harshly.

"Nothing, she never spoke at all. I asked her what she was called after I told her I was Candy, and when she didn't reply, I asked if she was going to speak or not. Then Hammer told me to leave." she tells me, blinking more than necessary.

"Okay, fuck off and tell Brandy to come in." I snarl, and she bustles out quickly, making me smirk at the sight.

I don't have to wait long before Brandy knocks and opens the door, "Come in," I say, then cross my arms over my chest. Once she's in the room, she closes the door, one of her ploys I've noticed, "Open the fuckin' door." I snarl but don't move from where I'm standing.

When Brandy has re-opened the door and turns to look at me, I quickly ask, "What happened when you took the meal upstairs to the woman?"

"When I went in, she was in the bathroom, and as she came out, she asked what I was doing, so I told her I brought her meal. Then she got aggressive, and Hammer came in and told me to leave." she gives me that nasty smirk she has. I know more happened than she's telling.

"Stay away from her when we bring her downstairs. If I see you bothering her, you're out the door. You got me, Brandy?" I snarl. She nods and rushes out.

I hope I get more information about what went on when Ruger has spoken to her. She'll have to leave if I don't get anything from her soon, which will put her in a risky position, especially if her ex finds her because from what I have seen, it's him that has caused all this.

CHAPTER SEVENTEEN

-:- CRACK -:-

After leaving the diner, we contacted Sharp and updated him on what we know so far. He thinks Raging Barons MC is keeping secrets but can't prove anything at this point. He gives us the address of the compound, and we head out that way before we start pounding the streets once more.

It's a lovely little town, and people don't seem afraid of us or our kutte. That tells us a story about the Raging Barons and the relationship they have with people around them.

We stopped to fill up our bikes. The people were friendly and told us without reservation where we could find Axel's club. That is how they refer to it, says much about Axel.

Riding up to the compound of the Raging Barons MC, we are met with a guarded gate, which we expected. Next to the entrance is a brick guardhouse. Now that did have my eyebrows raising.

"What can I do for you?" a young man with a prospect kutte on asks as he steps out of the guardhouse.

"We've come to speak to Axel if you can let him know Crack and four brothers are here," I state, leaning on my bike's tank with my forearms, stretching my back out a little.

"Hang on a few minutes, man." the prospect says, then makes a call from his cell while walking away so we can't hear what's being said.

We sit around a few minutes, and I'm looking at the clubhouse. It's a two-story building, excellent double door entrance, lots of windows, and the Raging Barons MC logo boldly painted on the wall.

The prospect heads back into the guardhouse and must hit a switch as we hear a buzzing, and the gate starts to slide open.

Starting my bike up, I slowly glide into the compound and park in a space near the double doors. The doors open, and three men step out, nodding at us to follow them in.

Inside the clubhouse, I have to admit it's in good repair, clean and tidy. People are sitting around, and all talking stops as we walk inside.

One of the brothers who brought us in has Buzz - Enforcer on his kutte and nods at us to follow him through the room and down a hallway to an office.

As we step inside, I see Axel sitting behind a desk, leaning back in his captain's chair, looking pretty relaxed.

"Please take a seat. You need a drink?" Axel asks.

"Yeah, a hot drink would be good for us, thanks," I respond before any of mine can ask for beer.

Buzz leaves the room, but I note another brother steps inside, obviously not willing to leave their President alone with us. His kutte states he is VP - Drag.

"So, how can I help you today?" Axel asks, steepling his hands on the desk and leaning forward.

"We've been following a lead to find Zara, Gunners' daughter, who we think is looking for Miriam Williams, who was in prison until recently," I state I'm not going to try and pull the wool over his eyes.

Axel keeps his gaze on me, "Yeah, know that much as Sharp has been in touch, but not sure what I can do for you."

"I wanted to check if you had any updates at all. We've just come from a diner that Miriam worked at but left for some reason." sitting forward in my seat, leaning my elbows on my knees.

"We have had no information about this girl, apart from she is with a man who was a Green Beret and is being kept safe," Axel states, still keeping his gaze on me alone.

Buzz re-enters the office carrying a tray with drinks for everyone. After handing them out, he stands on one side behind Axel.

Gunner starts to speak, and I turn sharply, "Shut the fuck up, you were told to keep quiet." and for once, he does as he's fucking told.

"We've been to this diner as I mentioned, and the woman told us that Miriam had been there working but had left, that she now goes by the name Mia," I take a sip of my coffee and keep my eye on Axel, "she said that she thought that Mia was set up by the woman she stabbed, which is Cara and I'll be honest with you I can believe it. The thing I don't know is why she would set her up?"

"Didn't you ever get to the bottom of this shit at the time, you know, before that woman was sentenced?" Axel snarls.

"Things were happening at the time, and a club was causing us issues, which kept us mostly away from the clubhouse and what was happening. Before any of us knew what was happening, she was in prison, done deal." I respond, giving Gunner a nasty look as I still think he could have dealt with all this differently.

"Shall I tell you what we heard, then and now?" Axel calmly asks.

"Yeah, you can tell us," I reply.

"We heard she was railroaded. That her ol' man deserted her without a hearing, he never asked her anything, not a fuckin' question."

Axel is getting on a roll, I can tell, and I'm thinking Gunner better keep his fucking mouth shut, "So how does it work that a woman has a kid, abandons her at the hospital, stays away for seven fuckin' years, then turns up and oh surprise gets stabbed by the woman who has been acting as this kid's mother without any incident for five years.

"This woman is instantly the guilty one?"

"Skank, however, has everyone believing she is innocent. Give me a break. It doesn't hold fuckin' water." Axel turns and stares at Gunner, he knows who he is, and he doesn't care either that what he's saying could set him off.

Gunner jumps to his feet and storms out of the office, and Axel nods at Buzz, who follows him out.

"You just said what we've all been sayin', we can't find Mia, or we could find out the truth. The girl was seven and hasn't said a single word to anyone since that day. I remember her trying to talk to her dad, and when he sent her to her room with her mother, she never spoke again." I inform Axel. "I want to talk to Zara too, see if I can get her to talk to me about what happened, but I've got to find her first."

"Well, we can't help you at the moment." Axel states and stands nodding at his VP to show us out.

I nod, "Thanks for your time. Here's my number if you hear anything, we'll be about trying to find Zara and Mia for a while yet. We can't stop looking for Gunner's daughter."

Leaving the compound, we head back towards town and a motel we'd seen on the way here. We need to talk seriously with Sharp and pound the pavement to find anything on this man and Zara's whereabouts.

CHAPTER EIGHTEEN

-:- MIA -:-

Pacing back and forth as I need to get out of here soon, I'm not used to sitting around all day; even in prison, they have you up early, busy all day, and then locked down early for the night.

All this waiting for something to happen and needing to get away from here is starting to wear pretty thin. Of course, the skanks bringing meals wearing next to nothing and smelling of beer and sex is not helping my attitude.

Hearing the lock on the door turn, I position myself, so I'm facing the door. These skanks are not getting my back. I learned about that in prison.

A tall man I've not seen before enters the bedroom, carrying a tray with a coffee pot with the fixings, plus some kind of cake but pretty misshaped and looks like someone sat on it.

He must be about six foot three, well built with short hair and beard, brown eyes that have a friendly look, rather than the cold eyes I've seen for years.

"My name is Ruger. Brought you a drink and not sure what that shit is but thought you might like something sweet," he says in a gravelly voice.

I nod but don't speak; that's what they are after me spilling everything. Maybe changing guys, they think, will loosen my tongue.

"Do you need anythin' else?" he asks, "Need any clothes washing?"

Still, I don't speak, standing firm and keeping my eye on him as he placed the tray on the dresser, turning to look at me once more.

He takes a step over to the bed and sits on the edge, giving me a nod to indicate I sit too.

I walk over to the window sill and take up the position I've had for the last few days. Looking out of the window at the men coming and going.

"Sharp's goin' to want to speak to you, Mia. We want to protect you and get the truth told. If we can do that, you can get your name cleared and some compensation to get your life back," he states in a calm voice.

Turning my head to look at him, I still don't speak, just take him in and the way he's giving me the friendly vibes.

That is how the next forty minutes are spent, him trying to talk me around and why I should open up to them, I can tell he's getting to the point he's going to walk, and I decide I'll say something.

"Do you have any idea what it's like working hard to get a career you love, to find the person that is supposed to be your everything and a daughter who, although is not blood, is loved as much as if they were?

 "When you're stabbed in the back, not given a chance to defend yourself and then thrown in prison with a sign on your back that at all cost, they should take you down.

"The person that put that sign on your back is the love of your life, or you thought they were. Any idea at all?

"Sharp and that club don't give a shit about the truth. They proved that, and if they come here, it's to get me back with them so they can take me out in a quiet place with no witnesses.

"So don't come in here giving me all your bullshit. It means nothing to me." and I turn back to the window and refuse to look or speak to him again.

Ruger leaves the room and quietly closes and locks the door, leaving me alone with my thoughts once more.

-:- ZARA -:-

After finding somewhere to pee, I settle back down next to Target, and we eat a protein bar and drink a can of soda. Target keeps his eye on the compound and listens to me talking about anything I feel like because I get bored quickly.

Target taps my shoulder and hands me his binoculars, and looking through them I see Crack, my dad, and three others entering the compound.

"That's my dad's club, and my dad is one of them. They must be looking for Miriam or me." I say to Target and hand him the binoculars back.

"Don't worry. We'll keep doing recon for now." Target says.

"What's recon?" I ask him, giving him all my attention.

"Reconnaissance means we watch them without them seeing us," he explains, and when I nod, he turns back to watching again.

"How long do we have to watch?" I ask as I've not done this spying before, and I don't know about his recon, but it's spying to me.

Target turns and sits on his butt, leaning on the tree behind us both, "Well, we have to see who is coming and going. If we can guess what's going on, we'll have a better chance of getting in there and getting out again safely."

"Okay," I lean against Target and rest my head on his shoulder, "I think Cara was doing something bad."

"What makes you think that?" he asks.

"She was using her cellphone to take pictures of papers at the clubhouse. She went in the office when Sharp wasn't around." I look up at him, "Someone called Snap kept calling her, and she was shouting at him. She couldn't see how much money the club had and what the numbers were."

"I knew where she's hiding the cell she uses when she talks to this man. I think they want to steal from the club."

"It sounds possible, Zara, but we need to tell them what's happening. Do you think you can do that? I'll be with you and won't let anything happen to you or anyone hurt you." Target asks as he's looking down at me.

"If you're with me, then I'll do it." I say, turning to look back across at the compound, "Do you think they're trying to find out what I know?"

"Probably," he responds, "They just want to find you and this woman you call Miriam. I don't know if they want to hurt her or not, but we haven't seen her here now, have we? Maybe she's still running."

We settle down again and carry-on spying. I have to smile a little as I know I was spying on people at the clubhouse, but maybe I was doing this recon Target talks about?

Around an hour later, my dad and the others leave the compound. They don't look pleased; maybe that means they didn't find anything out from the people in there.

"Can you stay here quietly while I go do some looking around? Be still, don't let anyone see you; we need to be unseen until we're ready to walk over and speak to them." Target states.

"Yes, I'll be quiet and stay here," I reply, and I settle back against the tree while I wait for Target to come back.

He must have been gone quite a while because I'd fallen asleep. As I open my eyes, it's dark and a bit spooky too. I sit up and can see the backpack because the moon is quite bright, so I take out a bottle of water and have a drink, then carry on waiting, but I'm getting scared Target has gone and left me or got caught by them across the road.

I'm just thinking I'll go over to the compound when I hear a noise behind me and turn to see Target coming out of the bushes.

"You okay, Zara? I was longer than I thought I would be, sorry about that," he says, smiling at me.

"I'm alright. Are you alright?" I hand Target a bottle of water and watch while he drinks the whole bottle, "I thought you weren't coming back."

"I wouldn't leave you on your own, Zara. I told you I'd look after you." he sits next to me, "There's a lot of men going in and out, I saw some women, but they don't look like the woman you talked about."

"You mean the club women, the nasty ones who don't wear clothes?" I ask, screwing my nose up.

"Yeah, those women," he smirks at me.

"Miriam isn't like that. She worked in a bank, and she had nice clothes, you know skirts and pants." I tell him, seeing her in my mind with her ponytail, pants, and white blouse.

"You can clear her name, Zara. Even if she doesn't want to go back to the club or be part of your life, you can clear her name, and that is the right thing to do." Target says, throwing his arm around my shoulders and wrapping us both up with the spare blanket.

"Yeah, I can, and I will. I just want to say I'm sorry," I tell him, "I don't want to live with Cara anymore. Do you think they'll make me?"

"If you tell them everything, I don't think she'll be at the club anymore, so you won't have to live with her. Also, you need to tell your dad or someone in charge that she hit you, and they won't let that happen once they know."

"Okay, Target, I'll do that as long as you're with me when I do it," I tell him.

"Come on, let's see if we can get some sleep. It's not cold, so we'll be okay until morning." Target settles down next to me, and I lay listening to an owl hooting and the music from across the road playing. It's not long before I'm fast asleep.

CHAPTER NINETEEN

-:- AXEL -:-

I know I've got to do something about Mia. I can't leave her in that bedroom for much longer, it's been five days now, and apart from the little she told Ruger, we've had no more information from her.

As I step out of the office, my cell rings, and I pick up the call. "Yeah." I snap out.

"Sharp here, I'm coming over. We'll be with you in about five hours. We need answers, and we know Mia and Zara are in your area somewhere, so we need to find them quickly. I've had enough of all this bullshit." he snarls back at me.

"What about the bitch who caused all this? What's happening to her?" I ask, knowing he can tell me to fuck off if he wants.

"She's in the cell in the basement, and when I get to the bottom of all this, I can decide what to do with her," he informs me.

"See you when you get here." I close out the call.

Things just took a more urgent turn, Mia has to open up now, or she'll be vulnerable to being taken back with Sharp. I can only protect her if she gives me the ammunition to do it.

Climbing the staircase heading to Mia's room, Drag follows me, "What's happening, Pres?" he asks.

"Sharp is on his way, we need information now, or we can't help her." and I open the door, stepping inside with Drag at my shoulder.

Mia is sitting on the window sill as she's been most of the time she's been here.

"Sharp is on his way, Mia. If you want our help, now is the time to tell us what we need to know. Otherwise, he'll be taking you back with him to his club, and we won't be able to stop it." I tell her, watching her reaction closely.

Mia steps away from the window, looks at us both, then picks up her backpack.

"Nobody listens to a word I say. Nobody believes a word I say. Can you give my belongings to Graham and Suzie at the diner, please? I won't live long once they get here, and I've nobody else." she says this calmly and resolutely.

Hearing her say this has my gut clenching. She's gone through so much and still has no one at her back as far as she sees it. After all we've said to her, she has no faith at all in anyone helping her.

I don't take the backpack, but I nod at Drag to follow me out. Once in the hall, I lock the door and run my hands through my hair, irritation running through me, not with her but with the situation.

Striding back down to the office, I slam myself down in my chair and look at Drag, who has a look of determination on his face.

"What the fuck are we gonna do, Drag?" I ask, "If she doesn't open up, we can't save her. Yeah, we can fight and tell them to fuck off, but what will that gain apart from a war we don't want."

Sitting in the chair in front of my desk, Drag places his forefingers on his temples, one of his tells when he's trying to work out a problematic situation.

Petey, one of the prospects, knocks on the door and asks if we need anything, and Drag tells him a pot of coffee, fresh and hot, to which he nods and runs off to fetch.

"Okay, Pres, let's think about this, we have option one, which is we go to war to keep her with us, if necessary, not an option we particularly want, but none of us will see an innocent woman murdered for something she never did." Drag states.

"Option two, we chuck her out so she can make a run for it, give her some time to get as far as she can before they catch her if they catch her.

"Option three, one of us claims her as an ol' lady, then they can do fuck all, and every man will stand up and have her back."

I'm shocked he thought of that, but it has merit and a lot of merits because he's right. If she's an ol' lady, every man will stand in front of her before they allow anyone to take her.

Trouble is convincing her to do the right thing, one way or another because telling everything that happened could still be the way out of this mess.

"Let's go have another word with our guest, shall we Drag?" I say, standing and heading back upstairs.

Opening the door to the bedroom, Mia walks out of the bathroom. She looks worn out even though she's done nothing but sit around in here.

"You have options, Mia. One, we go to war with your old MC to keep you safe, where some of us could get injured or killed for you, and you're not even club.

"Two, we cut you loose, and you make a run for it, hoping you get away, which is unlikely as you have no vehicle.

"Three, you become somebody's ol' lady, which makes you club, shows them they can't touch you, and everyone here will stand with you." I step towards her, "You've got an hour to make your mind up. They'll be here in three hours, so you'll still have a two-hour window if you decide to run."

Drag and I step out of the room and back down to the office. Sitting, we pick up the coffee that Petey left us. We look at each other questioningly.

"What do you think she'll do?" Drag asks.

"Fucked if I know." I admit, "I hope she goes for the last option as it'll make it easier, and we can push for fuckin' answers from them and that bitch who caused all this."

"Agree, and if she's an ol' lady once this shit is over, she can leave if she wants or stay depending on if she likes her ol' man or not." to which he laughs at his own comment, "Joking aside, she needs to be your ol' lady or mine, she's gotta be the ol' lady of a high up officer, or it won't work," he states. I nod as I agree with him.

"Do you want an ol' lady Drag?" I ask as I know he's always said he doesn't want to be tied down. Due to his parents, he's always against marriage or ol' lady for himself.

"Nope, so you're it, Pres, I don't want an ol' lady, you know that," he replies.

"Fuckin' hell, Drag."

I'm not sure what's going to happen, but we have less than an hour for Mia to make her mind up as to what she's going to do. Me, I would like an ol' lady, someone to share the day with, the bed at night and have some rug rats.

I've got to get this mess sorted out and moved forward, and if not with Mia, it's time I found my other half and settled down.

-:- CRACK -:-

Meeting up with Sharp and some of the brothers who traveled with him at a motel off the highway, we arrange to go straight to Raging Barons MC and find out what we can.

We need to find Zara and this guy and make sure she's safe, and he's not some kind of kiddy snatcher. The people we've spoken to sound positive about him, or I'd be apprehensive at this point.

Riding in formation, two of us, side by side, we make our way to the Baron's compound. I hope nothing untoward develops as Gunner is never far from throwing a temper, and Sharp isn't the calmest of men.

A prospect walks out of the guardhouse at the gate and picks up his cell to report we've arrived. Walking back inside, he hits the button that opens the electronic gate, and we head inside parking near the main doors.

Buzz, the Baron's enforcer along with another brother, meets us at the main door and guides us inside. Noticing the empty main room is a good sign that Axel has removed anyone not affiliated with the club.

Axel walks in and holds his hand out to shake with Sharp, and after that, we all take a seat. Axel points at the prospect behind the bar, and he starts pouring shots and beers while a brother hands them out, but I note he's taking stock of us as he does so.

After the usual welcome bluster is over with, Axel leans back in his seat and taps his knuckles on the chair arm, "So, what is it you want from us, Sharp?"

"We want help to find Zara, the young girl who is missing. Her dad Gunner is here, and they've been looking for days already," he responds and points out Gunner, but I'm sure Axel knows who he is from the last time we were here.

"We've had men out looking for over two weeks, so far they haven't seen her. We've had sightings but never had actual eyes on the girl." Axel states calmly.

"She's only twelve, has her birthday in two weeks, just a kid, too young to be out on her own," Sharp says to which Axel nods.

"So, tell me, any of you, why did a twelve-year-old feel she had to run away from home to find a woman that y'all had put behind bars?" Shit, not a good question. This will stir Gunner up.

I don't want this to get out of hand, so I lean forward, getting Axel's attention, "This is mainly on me. I've been trying to get Zara to talk to me about what happened and why she's been frightened at the clubhouse.

"I think I may have pushed her a bit too far, especially when I realized she wasn't goin' home but was hiding somewhere in the clubhouse.

"Then an incident happened with her mother Cara and the next day we couldn't find Zara, she just disappeared. We've been following her trail, and the trail leads her to Miriam, or Mia depending on what you want to call her. As yet, we haven't found Zara or Mia." I state, shaking my head.

"What do you want Crack? When you find either of them. What are your intentions?" Drag asks.

"The truth, after all this time, we want the truth," I lean back and cross my arms, "I never believed that Miriam hurt Zara. She loved that little girl, and she loved Gunner. But Cara is a different matter. She'd lie, cheat or steal if it would get her what she wanted."

Before anyone could say more, Gunner jumps up from his chair and storms over to me, and I'm ready for the prick. He can try if he wants. I'm not the enforcer of our club for nothing.

Sharp shouts, "Sit." Although Gunner wants to throw a punch, he refrains and sits back in his seat.

"I agree with Crack. Miriam was a good woman. She helped everyone; she worked in a bank, a clean-cut lass as my father used to say," Sharp places his ankle on his opposite knee and leans back in his seat, "Now Cara is another matter. I've always had my doubts about her but never had more than that, doubts, but she's in the cell at the minute, and Zip, our tech man, is digging up as much as he can about her, so I hope we have more answers soon."

"Well, it's taken you long enough to get to this point with her." Axel comments.

"Yeah, it has. When this happened, we were watching a rival club, Nameless Rebels MC. The leader is one of our brothers that we kicked out for stealing from the club. Snap had close to half a million dollars, and he ran before we could grab him. Had nothin' but trouble from him since." Sharp informs us.

Rogue enters the room and gives Axel a slight nod, not sure what that means, but Axel has a slight smirk on his face, worth watching, I think.

"I'm waiting for one of the brothers to come back in the morning. He's talking to someone who knows the man who is with your girl. If you get yourselves a motel for the night, then come back first thing we may have more news." Axel states and stands, letting it be known this meeting is done.

Turning, I shake Axel's hand, "Thanks for being so obliging. We'll return the favor if it's ever needed." and we make our way out and follow Sharp from the compound.

CHAPTER TWENTY

-:- MIA -:-

After Axel and his man leave, I sit on the bed with my back leaning on the headboard and rub my forehead. I don't know what I should do; this has all gotten out of control.

Three options, first, I can't allow the club to go to war for me if I have no ties to them. It just wouldn't be right. Two, do a runner, get as far as I can before they catch me, and then what, death? Three, become an ol' lady to one of these men? Shit, I never wanted to be involved with an MC ever again. If I become an ol' lady, will I ever get away again, doubtful I know?

I hear the lock, and the door opens. Then the skank walks in with a single cup. Yeah, she's up to something. I don't react at all, even when she stands staring at me.

"You want this drink bitch?" the skank asks, giving me an evil grin.

Who the fuck do these women think they are? They hardly dress, let men treat them like sexual doormats, and think they are special? It amazes me.

I continue to just look at her and wait for what comes next, but before anything can happen, a man walks in, grabs her by the back of her neck, and drags her out, all without a word.

The one they call Ruger walks in two minutes later, sits on the end of the bed, and looks directly at me.

"You've run out of time, Mia. Sharp and the brothers just pulled into the compound. We gave you as long as we could, so you're down to two choices, option one or three, two don't stand anymore."

Looking at him, I stand and walk to the window, looking down at the men that must have left the building and now sitting on the picnic benches talking.

"Okay, option three," I say just above a whisper.

"It'll be Axel, as he can give you the most protection," he states, sounding as though this is an everyday occurrence.

I nod as I don't know what I'm supposed to say.

"You okay with that, Mia?"

Again, I just nod but carry on looking out the window.

"Axel is goin' to get rid of them if he can. How he'll let them know you're his ol' lady, I don't know, but probably he'll keep it up his sleeve as an ace card when it's needed."

"Okay," I respond but say no more. What can you say when you're up against a wall?

"They will come back, and you'll have to tell your story, Mia. It'll have to come out eventually to clear your name and to get these fuckers off your back once and for all," Ruger says, "The more information you have, the more we can throw at them. Whatever you know about this, Cara will help. At the moment, she's in a cell as she was cruel to the daughter, and Crack caught her. All that goes for you Mia, it proves she has no love for the girl."

Again, I nod but say nothing. I know he's right. I'm going to have to speak up.

"I'll tell them what happened when they come back. But I won't go with them under any circumstances. If I leave with them, I won't live long." I tell him and look at him so he can see my truth.

Walking out, he speaks to whoever is on guard duty and then comes back in, handing me a bag.

"New clothes, wear them in the morning." and he closes the door and locks it as he leaves.

Waking the following day, I shower, wash my hair, and use the dryer that I asked the guard to find for me. Once I'm finished, I pace back and forth as I'm getting more and more worried about what is about to happen.

Looking in the mirror, I have to admit whoever got me the new clothes they at least purchased nice ones. The jeans are boot cut, a Harley t-shirt, and a blue sweater. The underwear matches and is in my size. How the heck they know all my sizes? I'm not sure. The ankle boots are black leather with a strap and buckle around the top of the ankle itself. At least I look decent in these clothes, and my hair is in a long braid.

The door opens, and Drag walks in, smiling at me as though we're old friends.

"Come on, Mia, follow me down, and once we're in the office, we'll get you some breakfast and a hot drink." he holds out his arm to indicate I lead the way.

We walk down the stairs and a hallway or corridor depending on where you come from and looking at Drag, he points to a door at the end.

Entering the room, Axel is sitting behind a desk, and as he sees us, he stands and signals for me to sit at the chair in front of the desk.

"What would you like for breakfast, Mia?" Axel asks.

"Whatever's handy, toast and coffee will be enough for me, thank you," I state. I'm not sure I could eat a lot with how things are because I feel sick already.

Axel looks over at Drag, "Get one of the women to get what Mia wants, watch them too, in particular Brandy."

Drag nods and leaves the office.

The room is quiet, and I'm not sure if I'm supposed to say anything or keep quiet, so I just sit and watch my hands in my lap.

"Are you okay about being my ol' lady Mia? You can be Drag's instead, but you have to be one of ours as our positions hold the most respect." Axel asks, sitting again behind his desk.

"It is what it is, and I thank you for helping me. Once this is all over, I'll make sure I walk away, and you can have a real ol' lady, one that will care about you properly, give you children." I state. I'm trying to let him see I'm grateful but will fuck off at the first opportunity I can.

"Well, we'll see what happens; only time will tell. For all purposes, you're my ol' lady, and you'll act like it and be treated like it." he looks directly at me, "Are we clear on that?"

"Yes."

Drag brings a tray and places it on the corner of the desk, a plate with toast and a coffee, plus sugar and cream.

Looking up, I give a small smile, "Thank you."

"Boss, we're gonna have to get rid of Brandy soon. Things are not right with that one. I caught her going to give Mia toast she'd rolled on the floor, but I made her eat the fucker." and he has a big grin on his face.

While eating, I keep quiet and listen to the conversation that Axel and Drag are having. Mainly about Sharp and where he stayed overnight, what they expect he'll do next.

"Are you up for the meeting with Sharp and his crew Mia?" Drag asks me, making me jump as I had let my mind wander.

"If you two are going to be with me, then yes, I'll tell what happened. But if Gunner is here, he won't believe me. He wouldn't even let me speak at the time." I tell them both.

"We'll be with you and more of the brothers. You've nothing to worry about. Just stay calm, keep your head up, be the ol' lady of the President." Axel says.

I nod, "I'll try to do my best."

We spend the next hour sitting in the office waiting for Sharp and his men to arrive, and I'm getting more and more nervous. Then I take a deep breath and think back to the time in prison when I was at my lowest when life didn't seem worth living, when I could have easily left this world without a backward glance, only to realize doing that gave them a win, and fuck if I was going to let them win.

CHAPTER TWENTY-ONE

-:- AXEL -:-

This meeting with Sharp went exactly as I expected. They're still blundering around, trying to find the girl and Mia. They're going to get a surprise when they come back.

Making sure we are all prepared for anything that may occur, we discuss in Church who will stay around inside the clubhouse and who will be monitoring outside.

The club women will be told to leave for the day, we don't want or need them involved, and the five prospects will be behind the bar or on the gate.

After making sure everyone knows what's happening and that I've claimed Mia as my ol' lady for the time being to give us leverage if they try and take her, we're all prepared and ready for whatever happens next.

After breakfast and the meeting in the office with Mia, I roam the main clubhouse room, dining area, and kitchen. My mind is full of *'what if's,'* but that's not my usual way of thinking, so I shake myself off and stand near the main door to wait for them to arrive.

Rogue walks over and stands beside me, "They're on the way. Rock's back from walking the streets, and they've had no sightings of the man or the girl."

I give Rogue a nod to let him know I heard but keep my eyes on the compound gate. I have a feeling not everything is how it seems, and some surprises are in store.

Hearing bikes, I walk away and back to the office, where Mia sits by the window. I stand next to her, "They're here, we'll come and get you when it's time. Be ready, be a Presidents' ol' lady." she turns to look up at me, "When this is done, you can choose if you want to stay an ol' lady and we'll make it work, or you can leave, the choice is yours." and I run my knuckles down her cheek gently, before turning and walking back into the main room.

The prospect brings me over a coffee as it's too early for alcohol, and I want a clear head, "Thanks, Jig, don't serve anyone alcohol. If they ask, the bar is closed on my orders."

Jig nods and walks back over to the bar, where he makes himself busy washing down and clearing away from the night before.

The main door opens, and Drag, Buzz, and Fox lead Sharp and his brothers into the room. I stand and nod to Sharp, who walks over and shakes my hand. Then we sit around the table, ready to start the talk.

"Okay, Rock has been into the town, talking to our contacts, and nobody has seen the man with your girl. If they're here, then they're keeping low to the ground." I take a drink of my coffee while I wait for two prospects to hand out pots of coffee and trays with cups and the fixings.

Sharp takes a drink and turns back to me, "Can your people have missed them? No disrespect Axel, I'm just trying to find out where to look next."

"No, my men miss nothing. If they're here in town, they're not staying in any motel or bed and breakfast houses. They are not even staying with the homeless community." I rub my forehead as I have the start of a headache, "The man your girl is with is an ex-

Green Beret, he'll know how to stay underground, not be seen, and he's been living as a homeless person, so has allies on the streets."

"Fuckin' hell, this just gets worse by the minute," Crack says, looking well and truly pissed off.

"The man has a good reputation. He's helped many in trouble on the streets. This is the intel I have from the street people. He stopped a girl from being raped, and he took an old lady home when she was lost, stayed with her until help arrived. There is more, but you get the idea." I state, "He's not gonna hurt your girl, but if he finds out you have, then he could hurt you."

Sharp stands, then paces back and forth a minute before throwing himself back into his chair. "Where do you think he'll be takin' her? Any ideas on that at all?"

"I think he's following the trail of where Mia went."

"Why? Because Zara wants to find her?" Gunner asks with some anger and resentment in his tone.

"Well, Gunner, yeah, I know who you are," I turn to him with my deadpan face, "You tell us why your daughter would run to a woman you put in prison rather than be with you and her mother?" Yeah, I put the fucker out there, fucking asshole is what he is.

Gunner jumps to his feet, "I don't know what's she thinking, fuckin' running off like this."

"If you stopped with your bullshit, you'd know why. We all know why and we don't even know any of you, but facts have a way of coming out." Turning to Ruger, I flick my eyes in the offices' direction. That's my tell to fetch Mia on my next tell.

Crack sits forward in his chair, placing his forearms on his knees, "Any chance you can share your intel, we need to find Zara before our enemies realize she's missing, my concern is for her, nothin' else."

"Let's find out some details, shall we before we jump onto anythin' else. Let's find out from Gunner what he thinks happened, because brother, I don't think he knows fuck all apart from a gut reaction that he was hurt at what he saw at that single moment in time." and I sit up and stare right at Gunner, a fucking jerkoff is what he is.

Sharp turns to Gunner and nods for him to speak up and tell what he knows.

Gunner stands, then takes a few paces and back again, trying to get his thoughts in order. While he's doing that, I notice Ruger walks out of the room. I know him. I know he's at the ready.

Gunner stops pacing and starts to talk, "Miriam came into my life when Zara was about two years old. We got along well right from the get-go. We met at a bar where she was drinking lemonade of all things with a couple of the women she worked with at the bank.

"She was the first woman I had met who wasn't a club whore, so she'd no idea who I was or anythin' about club life. It was refreshing not to be seen as a piece of club meat for the bitches I was usually around.

"We got together after a few months, and she moved into my house with my girl Zara and me. They seemed to get on well, and Zara learned a lot of things with Miriam teaching her.

"We were even talkin' about having a baby together when the shit hit the fan, and her true colors were shown.

"The day this happened, I had been on a run, just got back, was tired and ready for food and sleep. I walked into the kitchen and saw Miriam on top of Cara, who was screaming for help. When I pulled Miriam off, Cara had a blade stuck in her shoulder, and she was screeching that Miriam wouldn't allow her to see her daughter, which she had been trying to do for a long time.

"My vision blurred with anger, and I turned to Miriam and backhanded her across the face. Zara was screaming something. I don't know what. By that time, I was so livid I didn't see or hear anything else.

"I made sure Miriam was arrested and sentenced fast, taken out of our lives, and will be dead when I get my hands on her. Cara told me other shit that Miriam had been doing, so I made sure her life was hard in the pen.

"She pretended to love my girl, and that above everything was what had me instantly ready to kill her. She was a lying cunt and deserves everything she gets. Cara told me all that had been goin' on when I was on runs, hitting Zara and treating her bad."

"ALL LIES..." is said in a firm voice, having us all turn and see Mia standing with Ruger in the doorway.

Gunner lunges towards her, but I step in front of him, shoving him back, "You touch my ol' lady, and you're a dead man."

The room is instantly silent, and Gunner gives Mia death glares, which she's not responding to. She has her head up as I told her. She's being the Presidents' Ol' Lady and acting it well.

I hold my arm out, and thankfully Mia takes the clue and walks to me, bobbing under my arm, and I wrap it around her shoulders. The fact she is much smaller than me helps.

Sharp stands, running his hand over his hair, "Fuckin' hell, this is a mess. You never told us she was your Ol' Lady Axel."

"No, I didn't, because it's not your fuckin' business. My club has nothin' to do with you, except you give us the respect we give you." I state blankly. He can kiss my ass.

The murmurs, cursing, and growling in the room quietens after a few minutes, and my brothers are standing around the room at the ready. The visiting brothers all look pissed, but at who, I'm not sure.

"Mia, sit next to me and tell your story," I say, and gently seat her, but keeping myself ready to jump up if needed.

"I met Gunner as he stated, we hit it off well, I liked him. We laughed a lot, had good conversations about everything you can imagine, from politics to paintings.

"When I met Zara, she was two, a pretty little girl who needed a woman around her. She had many uncles, and they all loved her, but the only females were club skanks who didn't care about her at all.

"The only thing I knew about Cara was that she gave birth to Zara, then walked out of the hospital and was never seen again. I never met her, saw her, or spoke about her with or to anyone, so when she turned up that day, I was so surprised I didn't react for a moment.

"She burst into the kitchen wielding a knife, screaming about she needed to be back in the club, she needed information for her Ol' Man, she hated Zara and wished she never had her and that she was going to end her. She lunged at Zara with the knife, and I rushed to stand in front of her, taking a slice of the blade across my upper arm. Then I grabbed her arm, and we struggled. I shouted at Zara to get out of the kitchen and find someone to help.

"When I looked at Zara, she was frozen to the spot, terrified, I think. So, I shouted at her again to get help, still struggling with Cara.

"Then I managed to get the knife from Cara, and she lunged again, we fell to the floor, I don't know how but the knife was in her shoulder.

"That's when Gunner came into the kitchen and my life as I knew it ended. My life was ruined saving his   daughter."

Everyone started talking at once; disbelief, shock, and anger rushed through the room. Gunner is standing staring at Mia, still in a deadly manner.

Sharp stands from his seat and turns to Gunner, but before he can say anything, Gunner starts to shout, "You're a lying whore."

We all turn to the door when we hear a small voice say, "No, she isn't, she told the truth." and standing there is Zara and a man we don't know.

CHAPTER TWENTY-TWO

-:- ZARA -:-

Waking this morning, I'm ready to go home and to have a real bed, but I still have to find Miriam and tell her I'm sorry. I don't know if she'll forgive me, but I have to tell her anyway.

I go into the bushes to do my morning pee, then take a few wipes to clean up everywhere. I don't like showers that much as I like lying in the bath, but a shower would be good about now.

We eat a protein bar and open a can of soda, watching the morning activities at the compound, turning to Target, "Are we still doing recon? You know spying on them?"

Target grins finishes his can, and looks to the compound, "My gut tells me something is about to happen. We'll make our move when it does. We get in, you tell your truth, and if needed, we get out again. Whatever happens, I'll keep you safe."

Nodding at him, I smile as I know he will. He's kept me safe all this time.

A few minutes later, we see a stream of bikes ride up to the compound gate, speaking to the prospect who opens it for them and quickly closes it again once they are through.

Target turns to me, "Let's pack up, Zara. We're gonna be moving in a short while."

It doesn't take us long to fold the blankets, place all the empty wrappers, cans, and bottles into the bag that Target had at the ready and tuck the backpacks and carryall against the tree for when we come back for them.

"Are you ready to go put all this right?" he asks, looking down at me, then tucks some hair behind my ear.

Nodding, "I'm ready."

We walk over to the compound and stand, waiting for the prospect to come out of the guardhouse and speak to us.

"What can I do for you?" the prospect asks, and I'm surprised he asks in a friendly way too.

"I need to speak to Sharp, the President of Rogue Legion MC. I know he's here as I saw him come here a while ago." I tell him and hope he doesn't argue.

"What are you called, and I'll see what I can do," he asks, taking out his cell.

"My name is Zara Michaelson. I'm Gunner's daughter." I state strongly.

The prospect walks a little away, speaks to someone, then returns to us, nodding as he enters the guardhouse and opens the gate.

As the gate opens, my stomach does a flip flop. I'm nervous. In fact, I'm scared. I look up at Target, and he gives me the nod and squeezes my shoulder, keeping his hand there to provide me with courage.

Someone walks out of the building, and Target guides me slightly behind him, giving the man a good look as we get near him.

"Names Hammer, follow me inside. A meeting goin' on, so you need to go in quiet-like," he states, giving me a weak smile.

Target and I nod that we understand, and we enter the building. I hear part of what my dad is saying, then what Miriam says. Before I can say anything, at that point, my dad calls her a lying whore.

"No, she isn't. She told the truth." I say, but it comes out reasonably quietly as I'm scared.

My dad sees me, and anger is rolling off him. He storms towards me, "Where the fuck have you been, worrying everyone, causing shit?"

He's coming at me full-on, furious; you can see it in his face, but before he gets to me, Target steps in his way and shoves my dad back hard.

My dad throws a punch, but Target spins, lift his leg and kicks my dad in the chest, which has him flying backward and hitting chairs and a table behind him.

Target pulls an arm back, gently pushes me behind him, and moves us both back, so the wall is behind me and Target is in front.

My dad flies once more toward Target, hitting him in the stomach with his shoulder, and I rush to the side to get out of the way as they both fly towards the wall.

Target hits my dad on the back of his head with his elbow and takes him down to his knees.

Two men rush over and grab my dad, pulling him across the room and slam him down in a chair. Then they stand next to him, with each of them holding him with a hand on his shoulder.

Sharp calmly walks over to me, keeping one eye on Target, who's still standing slightly in front of me. He reminds me of Trip's attack dog when he's guarding something.

"Are you alright Zara?" Sharp asks, coming to a stop a couple of steps in front of Target.

"Yes, thank you. Target is my friend, and he looked after me." I state as I don't want anyone hurting him, "I've been looking for Miriam so I can tell her I'm sorry."

"Sorry for what, Zara?" Sharp asks as he squats down in front of me.

"For not making anyone listen, I could have made someone listen, I could have stood in the clubhouse and shouted at the top of my voice that she didn't do anything wrong, but I didn't because when I tried, my dad wouldn't listen, no one was listening, so I stopped talking at all." I blurt out, and tears start tracking down my cheeks.

"Cara has been lying to you all for a long time. She's been telling a man what you have all been doing, where you've been going.

"She doesn't want to be with us at the club. She has another club she wants to be with." I blurt out.

Sharp steps back and picks up a chair, placing it in front of another, then he sits and points for me to sit facing him.

"Tell me it all, Zara," he says, giving me a weak smile.

Target stands behind me and places one hand on my shoulder, squeezing it, "Now's your time, Zara, tell him it all."

Dad shouts, "Get you hands off my daughter."

Target places his hands over my ears, then I hear a muffled, *"Fuck off, cocksucker."*

Looking at Sharp, I take a deep breath, "Cara came back because her ol' man told her she had to. She has to get the information about your money. He wants her to get the numbers.

"I think he means the bank account numbers, but I'm not sure. She speaks to him every Friday when dad is at the clubhouse or somewhere other than the house.

"Well, dad never comes home anymore, so he doesn't know what is happening at home anyway."

Sharp nods, giving dad a look, I don't recognize, "Anything else, any names at all?"

"She called him Snap, and he's her ol' man, not my dad." the room erupts with anger, so I think they recognize the name, "I have this," and I dig into my backpack, right to the bottom and find the cell that she hides, which I stole when I left. I pass it to Sharp, "She uses this to call him every Friday as I told you."

I stand and walk toward Miriam, who is not looking at anyone, but down at her knees. "I'm sorry, Miriam. I wish I'd told them sooner, made them listen." I start to cry, and Miriam stands, places her hands around my shoulders, and whispers so no one else can hear, "It's okay, none of it's your fault. I'll always love you." and she kisses the top of my head and steps away.

I know that's the end, as I can feel it. She won't be coming home with us. She won't be the mother I always wanted. Walking over to Target, I put my arms around his waist and cry. He pats my shoulder, knowing too that I lost Miriam.

Sharp stands, pats my shoulder too, then turns to the room, "We need to get back, find out what the fuck is goin' on with Cara. We all know Snap. We know he's been tryin' to take our business and take the club down since we kicked him out. Her being his ol' lady means nothin' to us, but we need her confession so we can clear Miriam's name."

"No, we'll do that," Axel says, and I lean on Target, not knowing what will happen to him.

I tug on his sleeve, and when Target looks down at me, "What are you goin' to do Target, are you coming home with me?"

Squatting in front of me, Target looks me right in the eye, "No, it's not my home. I'm not sure where it is, but your club isn't it. But I'll always be your friend, and if you need me, you just have to call me." he turns to Axel, "Do you have a cell I can buy from you so I can give Zara a number to call if she ever needs me?"

Axel nods at one of his men, who rushes out of the room to return a few minutes later and passes Target a cell, then hands me a piece of paper with the cell number on it.

Tears flow as I look at Target, knowing he'll be going soon and I may never see him again.

Axel steps towards us, "Target, you're welcome to stay with us, join us, we do a lot of good things, and you may find your place here. Stay awhile and see if you think you can fit before you make a decision."

I walk over to my dad, "Are you going to listen to me now? I don't want to go home with you if you're going to be with Cara; she is horrid. She hits me when you're not home. I'll stay with Crack before going back to Cara."

Standing, my dad wraps his arms around me and kisses my head, "I'm so very sorry, Zara, I'll do better with you, I promise." then he steps towards Miriam, who instantly moves behind Axel, "I'm sorry Miriam, I'll find out the truth and make it right."

Stepping to the side of Axel, Mia gives an ugly laugh, "You'll make it right, you'll give me back five years of my life, the misery and hurt. I want nothing to do with you ever again."

Gunner drops his head, and for the first time, shows shame for what he's done and the pain he's caused.

Sharp thanks Axel and shouts to his men that they're leaving.

I hug Target again, and he runs a finger down my cheek, smiling at me, "It'll be okay little girl." and as I leave, I hope it's not the last time I'll ever see him.

CHAPTER TWENTY-THREE

-:- CRACK -:-

Back at our clubhouse, I see Gunner and Zara trying to act naturally towards each other, but it's going to take some work on Gunner's part to put things right between them. Quite a bit of damage was caused thanks to Cara and her lies.

Cara, now that is someone, I'm never happy to see, and she won't be happy to see me either. I've never been into hurting women, but this one I don't think is a decent human being, so I have no issue with making her hurt if needed.

Zip is checking out the cell that Zara gave us, looking at all the messages and the amount of incoming and outgoing calls. Hopefully, he'll get enough information to show us how much she'd been spying and for how long.

Once everyone has gathered in Church for the meeting, Sharp has called. I lean against the back of my chair and am pleased I brought this forward all those weeks ago. I just wish I'd done it much earlier.

Calling the meeting to order, Sharp smacks the gavel on the table and looks around to make sure everyone is here.

"Okay, as you all know, we have new information regarding Miriam, who, by the way, goes by Mia these days. She is innocent of what she was accused of and sadly has done five years we can't give her back," Sharp sits forward and leans on the table, "We know that Mia saved Zara from being stabbed by Cara."

The room rumbles with disgust, and some are throwing nasty looks at Gunner, and he's going to have to live with that.

Trip sits back in his seat, "What we have found is Cara is not Gunner's ol' lady because she is the ol' lady already for Snap of Nameless Rebels MC."

The room again erupts, this time with more venom, and calls to take out the Nameless Rebels once and for all.

Glue taps his knuckles on the table to get attention, "Did you find the man that was with Zara? Was she safe with him?"

I respond to Glue's question, "He looked after her and continued to do so right up to the moment we left the Baron's clubhouse to bring Zara home. You can tell by his stance he's ex-military, he has the aura, and he wasn't afraid to throw down for Zara against any of us."

The shock around the room would be comical if it weren't something that set Gunner off again.

"Fucker, he'll get what's coming," Gunner snarls.

Sharp bangs his fist on the table, hard, "You'll keep your head down, look after your daughter, and sort your fuckin' life out. Or you'll be giving me your patch. It's time you pulled your hot head out of your ass and checked what's goin' on around you. You'll not touch that man, he made sure Zara was safe, and we owe him for that. She could have been in a fuckin' kiddy ring, or Snap could have grabbed her."

Knocking on the door and Zip walks in, "Sorry to be late comin' in Pres. I wanted to finish checking that cell, and it clearly shows messages between Cara and Snap for years. He plays her for what he wants, although she is his ol' lady.

"It shows arguments they have because he's not faithful to her, and she hates that, although she slept and had a kid with Gunner, on Snap's command.

"Snap wanted her to have a kid, so she had a solid *in* with the club, kept suspicion off her. She hates Zara from the messages I've read and would have hurt her given a chance.

"He wanted information on our bank accounts and the account numbers so he could drain us dry. When I checked the cameras, I looked at your office cameras, and she's been in looking at anything you left on the desk and unlocked drawers."

The grumbles, snarls, and cursing in the room reflects how everyone feels about Cara and Snap.

"Time to take out the garbage Pres, what do you want us to do?" I ask, keeping one eye on Gunner too.

"Let's go down and have a little talk with Cara. Crack, Trip and Tin, with me." Sharp states, "Meeting closed for now, but stay in the clubhouse because I'm sure we're gonna have another meeting."

Gunner jumps onto his feet, "Am I coming with you to talk to Cara?"

"Not at this time, you stay here, talk to your daughter, make sure she's okay," Sharp responds, "If I need you, I'll let you know."

In the basement, Cara is sitting on the only chair in the room, an old dining chair, so not very comfortable. To say she's been down here days, she doesn't look too bad for it. Sleeping on the concrete floor must have been cold, but I don't give a shit.

"What's goin' on? Why am I still in here?" Cara whines.

Sharp stands in front of her, arms folded over his chest, "We have your cell that you contact Snap with," She jerks with shock, "Yeah, we know what you've been up to, we know you're his ol' lady, and we know you're a fuckin' traitor to this club."

I have to smile as she drops her head and closes her mouth. Now she knows she can't lie to get out of it.

Stepping near to her, I ask, "Why did you set Miriam up? Why hurt your daughter when you didn't need to? She never did anything wrong to you."

"She was born." Cara snarls.

I look over at the others, and they're shaking their heads in disgust.

"What did Snap have planned?" I continue.

She tries to keep quiet, but I'm sick of this bitch, so I pinch her arm.

She squeals and starts sputtering, struggling to stand but must have forgotten that Trip had tied her to the chair.

"What is Snap after? What has he planned?" I ask again. Cara says nothing, staring at the floor, I didn't want to get physical with her, but it looks like I may have to.

Gunner walks through the door even though he was told not to by Sharp, I glance at Sharp, and he pinches his lips together but doesn't comment.

Gunner walks over to Cara, grabs her hair, and yanks her head back hard, "So bitch, you thought you could hurt my daughter and laugh that you put an innocent woman behind bars."

Cara surprises me as she burst out laughing, sounds like a witch's cackle, and has the hairs on my arms standing on end.

"Snap will kill you all. He's going to take you all out, then take your clubhouse and live on your earnings and hard work." Cara once again cackles, and before any of us can do or say anything, Gunner shoots her between the eyes.

We all turn and look at Gunner as we can do nothing about Cara now. She's dead and good riddance if you ask me.

"Sorry Pres, but she wasn't worth saving," Gunner says, then turns and walks out.

Sharp shakes his head, looks at Cara, who's draped forward but still strapped to the chair, and grins.

"Hated the bitch, good riddance to her, hope she rots in hell where she belongs," Sharp states, then walks out shouting a prospect to come and get rid of the garbage. It's a good thing we have a large acid bath at the back of the property.

Back upstairs, Sharp calls everyone back into Church, quickly updating the details regarding Cara and her being dead. Also, the takeover bid Snap wants.

"We know where they are Pres, let's just take them out on one of the nights they throw a party, then boom the lot of them. Even the women that party with them are just skanks of the worst kind. I know we don't normally hurt women but come on, if they want these men, they're worthless." Trip states, rubbing his hand down the back of his neck.

I stand, "Can we call a vote, Pres? Let's get it done."

Sharp nods, puts it to the vote, and we make our plan to take the Nameless Rebels MC out of service.

CHAPTER TWENTY-FOUR

-:- AXEL -:-

Sharp and his crew have left, and the clubhouse has calmed down once more. The aggression was building mainly because of Gunner and his damn temper. He needs to get a hold of that before he has issues with his daughter.

"Are you okay, Mia?" I ask, placing my arm around her shoulder and bringing her into my body.

Giving me a nod, I hear Mia sniffle and look down, pushing her away from me slightly. I can see she's crying, "Come on, let's go to the office and calm down a little."

As we walk away, I wave my arm at Target and indicate he follow us. In the office, I sit Mia in the chair behind the desk, then sit on the corner of the desk.

Looking over at Target, I nod for him to sit, and once he's settled, I ask, "Would you like to stay here with us a while, Target? You don't have to prospect if you just need a time out after looking after Zara."

Sitting upright, Target places his ankle on his knee, claps his hands behind his knee, and looks directly at me, "I've been living on the street a few months, had a bad time when I lost most of my team. Only one other is still alive. We keep in touch. Zara walking over to me and asking for help seemed to snap me out of the shit I was stewing in.

"She's a sweet girl, cares a lot about you, Mia, and she cried numerous times that she hadn't done more to clear your name. It seems to me she was ignored and had to raise herself from what she told me.

"Her mother is a real piece of shit, and I hope they take her out. If not, I'm sure I will at some point. If she hurts Zara again, she won't breathe long afterward.

"I hope, given time, you may be able to have a friendly relationship with Zara, I know you care about her, it's easy to see, and it would be so sad if you both lose each other.

"I would like to stay a while if that's okay. See how things work here. If I like the look of it, like the brotherhood, then I may just prospect and draw my teammate in too."

I pick up my cell and message Dice to come and collect Target, get him settled in a room, and anything he may need, be it clothes or food.

"One of the brothers will take you to your room. If you need anything, all you have to do is ask, and we'll get it. Just hang out, meet the brothers, talk, learn and rest, then we'll talk again." I tell him, shake his hand and watch him leave the office with Dice, who I can hear talking his ear off already.

Turning to Mia, I'm a little worried as she has been so quiet, "Are you alright, Mia?"

Lifting her head to look at me, she gives me a weak smile, "Yes, I'm good, just shocked that after all this time, the truth has been told and the lies uncovered."

Nodding in agreement, I step up to her and hold my hand out, which she looks at for a moment, then places her hand in mine, standing. She is about a foot shorter than I am, and as I look down and she looks up, I can feel some heat in her gaze, but now is not the time to push my luck.

"Have you decided what you want to do, Mia? Do you want to stay here a while, rest, recuperate from all this shit," I stroke my finger down her cheek, "Do you want to leave straight away, move on and not look back? Or do you want to stay, be my ol' lady, letting us build something good?"

Mia studies my face, and for the first time, I see something in her eyes, not sparkling but not dead as they have been since she arrived here.

"Firstly, I want to thank you for wanting to know the truth. I know we can do nothing to change what happened, but it's a relief knowing that someone cared enough to even look at what happened," Mia smiles a little more, "Can I stay for now and think about what you're offering? Get to know you all more because I vowed I would never get mixed up with another MC."

"Yeah, that's perfectly fine. You can stay in the same room, but without being locked in." smirking at her this time.

We spend the rest of the day talking and meeting the brothers as they are in and out of the clubhouse. I take her for a walk around the compound, and she meets Jig, who is the prospect on the gate today. We should have called him Joke as he is always upbeat and willing to play a joke on someone or be on the receiving end of one.

The club women were warned that one step out of line and they'll be out the door fast. Buzz delivered that message, and they all know not to mess with him.

I have to smile because after Buzz had given them the 'talk,' they veered around Mia wherever she went, making sure they didn't give her eye contact.

Target has taken to talking with Mia often, they have spoken of Zara and the discussions he'd had with her, and I'm pleased to know Mia has no bad feelings for her, just sadness that she never tried to do more even though she was young.

A week after Sharp and his brothers had gone home, he contacted me to tell me that Cara was dead. They had uncovered a lot of information on her being a traitor and that Snap was up to his neck in terrible shit; even trafficking was mentioned.

A few days after that conversation with Sharp, he contacted me again to tell me that the Nameless Rebels MC was no more. I'm thankful to hear that as we were going to be looking into the trafficking comment to see how much truth there was to it.

Things were settling down nicely, and my daily routine was back to normal, making sure the nightclub we owned was running smoothly, and the bar we were looking into purchasing was solid, which would give us an additional business in the next town.

Target knocks on the door and pops his head into the office, "Come in. How can I help you?" I ask him as he stands in front of my desk.

"I've decided I'd like to prospect depending on how long that role takes. I'm not sure I want to be at everyone's beck and call for over a year. I did that once and don't want to do it again." he tells me, and I'm pleased by his honesty.

"Okay, I'll tell you if you want to prospect you do no more than a year, that I can guarantee," I tell him as I think he most likely will only do six months.

Nodding in agreement, I give him a handshake and a slap on his back, then bellow for PT to get himself in the office and get our new prospect set up and on the schedule of gate duty and anything else needed.

After Target leaves the office, I have a smile on my face as I'm pleased that he's going to stay and give it a chance. I think he'll be one hell of a brother once he's settled in. He also speaks of a team member who he thinks will prospect if he decides to, and that would mean the club gains two excellent brothers given time.

I look up when a soft tap gets my attention. I see Mia standing in the doorway, giving me a small smile, "Can I come in?" she asks.

"Of course, come in. What can I do for you?" I say, looking her over.

Walking in, Mia comes and stands next to my chair, looking down at me with a look I've not seen on her face before.

"I've made a decision Axel," she says in a soft voice, and I stand as a bit of anxiety hits me.

"Tell me, what have you decided?" I ask nervously.

"I've decided after meeting everyone, talking with Target about Zara, and watching how you are with everyone here that I would like to stay. I'd like for us to get to know each other, Axel. I'm not saying I'm ready to jump into bed with you, but I would like us to go out, spend time together, get to know each other. I'd like to be a part of the club and be your ol' lady, but I just need a little time for us to take that last step." she quickly says, as though she has to get it out before she forgets to say it all.

"I'm happy with that, Mia, and we can take our time." smiling at her and relieved she had made this decision.

"Do you think you could do something for me?" Mia asks."

"Yes, just ask."

"Will you kiss me?" she says, fucking right I'll kiss her, and that is precisely what I do.

Smiling down at her, I rub my thumb along her bottom lip and whisper, "Between us, we'll always have the truth. Between us, we never tell lies." she smiles, then reaches behind my head to draw me back down for a kiss that seals our fates.

*** Axel and Mia's story continues in the Raging Barons MC series***

BOOKS BY J.E. DAELMAN

SATAN'S GUARDIANS MC

Book One - Brand

Book Two - Shades

Book Three - Odds

Book Four - Torch

Book Five - Ace

Book Six - Nash

Book Seven - Ink

Book Eight - Shadow

Book Nine - Christmas at the Clubhouse - Novella

Book Ten - Whisky

RAGING BARONS MC

Prequel - Truth and Lies

President - Axel - Book Two

Silver - Book Three

Fox – Book Four

Grease – Book Five

Hammer – Boos Six

BS – Book Seven

ACKNOWLEDGEMENTS

Firstly, thanks to Richard, who Alpha/Beta reads and Edits, you work so hard and I'm so grateful for all you do.

Thanks to my Alpha Reader on this book, Marie.

For my Beta readers, Karen, Sue, Vic, and Emma.

My ARC team, you all keep me tapping the keyboard, giving me the confidence to carry on and enjoy my imagination. Thank you for each, and every review you write; every word means such a lot to me.

Lastly, thank you to my readers, who have reached out and given so many lovely comments about the books, especially your laughter about the old boys and their antics. I also thank you for the stunning reviews you place. Each one encourages a new reader to give the books a try ♥

~~*~*

You can find me here:

Facebook Author page:
https://www.facebook.com/Jan.SGMC

Facebook Reader page:
https://www.facebook.com/groups/335434258378835

Twitter:
https://twitter.com/daelman_author

Instagram:
https://www.instagram.com/jandaelman_author/

MeWe:
https://mewe.com/i/jandaelman

Blog:
https://jdaelman-author.blogspot.com/

Goodreads:
https://www.goodreads.com/author/show/21391970.Jan_Daelman

BookBub:
https://www.bookbub.com/authors/j-e-daelman

SIGN UP FOR THE NEWSLETTER

https://www.subscribepage.com/u9r7b4